Can't

Depend

on

MURDER

Jay Heavner

Canaveral Publishing

Cover design by Chris Stanley

Fineline Printing, Titusville, Florida

All the author's books can be obtained at Amazon

Braddock's Gold Novels

Braddock's Gold

Hunter's Moon

Fool's Wisdom

Killing Darkness

Florida Murder Mystery Novels

Death at Windover

Murder at the Canaveral Diner

Murder at the Indian River

Murder at Seminole Pond

Murder of Cowboy Gene

Murder in the Family

Murder the Most Dangerous Game

Going to the Dogs

Can't Depend on Murder

Dedication

To

Patches

My lap buddy and therapy cat.

I miss you, little girl.

Acknowledgments

Special thanks to my wife, Vivian

for suggestions, proofing, support, and edition.

Thanks, William Rowland for first proofing.

To all my first readers,

Sam Rizzo,

Lora Sargent,

Sandy Anne Smith,

Rene Hunt,

Marie Waters Clyne,

Cindy Moran,

Janice Carey,

Ann Tayloe,

and,

Ashley Marang

Can't Depend on

MURDER

Chapter 1

Late Spring 1988

Who's sittin' on my porch? The hair on the back of his neck
stiffened. His throat tightened. He relaxed when he realized the
stranger was the Shaman, the odd Seminole medicine man, who
lived in the marshes along the St. John River in Florida. He had a
way of showing up at the most curious and inconvenient of times,
and lately, when he appeared, nothing good followed.

The drive from the nearby town of Cocoa had been
uneventful, but when Roger stopped in front of his trailer to open the
gate, he'd noticed someone in a chair on his screened-in porch. He

drove to his old trailer and got out. "Hello, Shaman. Make yourself at home, why don't you?"

The Shaman said nothing.

Roger opened the porch screen door, went in the trailer, got two beers, and sat down next to the Indian. "Want a beer?"

"No."

"Some ice tea?"

"No."

"Can I get you anything?"

"No."

Roger grunted, "So, Shaman, what brings you here? Seems when you show up, something's always about to happen."

"The Ancient Ones speak from pond. When you tell their story? They impatient. If you dead, their story not get told. They say you must be one tell it. Beware, Roger Pyles. Danger."

"Yeah, but that's behind me. I solved that problem."

"No, more. Waiting. Be careful. Dead men tell no tales. Beware, Roger Pyles, if you want to live. Beware."

"Of what?"

The Shaman opened his mouth to speak, but closed it. He got up quickly, left saying nothing, leaving a startled Roger. He'd no more disappeared into the swamp brush when a large black vehicle stopped in front of his trailer. A commanding voice came from its loudspeaker, "Roger Pyles, stay where you are. We need to talk."

Roger yelled, "Who are you, and what do you want?"

"Brevard County Sheriff English. We have business. I'd like to speak with you."

"Sure. Come on down."

No one got out of the big vehicle, and the engine continued to run. K9, his dog, came out from under the trailer and growled.

"I agree with you, girl. Something smells funny. Maybe he didn't hear me, but if whoever it is wanted to shoot me, they could have done it by now."

K9 growled again.

Roger rose from his chair, waved his arms, and motioned for them to come on down. A moment or two passed before the engine of the vehicle shut off. Three doors opened and two large men in green uniforms wearing police duty belts with all the normal equipment and some Roger was unfamiliar with, got out. They looked around suspiciously and then said something to someone in the vehicle. A moment later, a broad-shouldered man of medium height exited. He, too, was dressed similar to the other two men, but he wore spectacles, not the dark sunglasses like the other men.

They walked to the gate. The two larger men's heads deliberately swung from side to side, searching.

Roger yelled, "The gate's dummy-locked. Come on down, and we'll talk."

The shorter man gave him a thumbs-up, fidgeted with the lock and chain, opened the gate, and they came through it.

Roger hollered, "Secure the gate or my donkey will get out."

The last man in the procession did so, and they walked toward Roger's old trailer. A noise to the left sent hands to their5 guns. Donkey trotted in their direction.

Roger shouted, "Pay no attention to my donkey. He's just curious. He won't harm you."

Donkey slowed his pace and walked up to the sheriff, who held his hand out. Donkey sniffed it, and the sheriff took his head in

3

his hands and stroked it gently. After a few rubs, Donkey turned and walked away slowly. The men proceeded to the old trailer.

When they got near, Roger said, "I'm Roger Pyles, but I think you knew that, or you wouldn't be here. Won't you come in, take a seat, and we'll talk turkey?"

"Thank you, Mr. Pyles," the shorter man said as he opened the door to the screened-in porch. "I'm Brevard County Sheriff Wayne English." He held out his hand, and Roger shook it. "This is Deputy Sandman and Deputy Ellifritz." The two men nodded.

Roger said, "I've got a chair for me and one for you, Sheriff. I can get two more for the Deputies."

"That won't be necessary, Mr. Pyles, but thank you."

"Make it Roger. Mr. Pyles is too formal."

"Very well, Roger. Guess you know why I'm here."

"You're selling tickets to the Policeman's Ball."

The sheriff smiled. "That's an old one I haven't heard in a while. I was told you could be a jokester. I like a man with a sense of humor. With all the troubles a cop sees, it's good to still be able to laugh. You know what I'm here for, right?"

Roger said, "That's a leadin' line used to get a suspect to confess."

The sheriff smiled. "Yes, I guess it is." He stopped. "You probably have heard about the women's bodies that turned up along I 95."

Roger nodded, "I have. Rumor has it there's a serial killer on the loose, your agency has been able to turn up little, and you're looking for outside help."

"True, Roger. I've heard of your abilities, and you come highly recommended by certain people in my department and

4

elsewhere. I was hoping you'd take a look at what we have and consider heading up an investigation. I can supply you with all the information we have and assure you that you will have the complete cooperation of my department."

"Won't some of your investigators be upset you're goin' outside for help?"

"Normally they would be, but we're so busy and understaffed, they're the ones who suggested it, and your name came to the head of the list of candidates."

Roger said, "I'm interested. I won't say yes or no to taking the case without further consideration. And tell me something. Why are these other two men here? Bodyguards?"

"They are. Some people would like to see me dead, and there have been attempts on my life."

"Yeah, I can understand that. It's not a good feeling. Will I have the complete files and papers of evidence you have?"

"I have them in our vehicle. I wanted to make sure you'd agree."

Roger shifted and looked the sheriff eye to eye. "I said I'd look. After I see the files, I'll let you know."

"I was hoping you'd take it, but I can understand your hesitation." He turned to one man. "Sandman, I need you to get the files and folders and bring them to Roger."

"As you wish." The big man exited the porch and headed for the vehicle parked on the shoulder of Canaveral Flats Boulevard.

"There is one more thing."

"What's that?" the sheriff asked.

"This came yesterday." Roger handed him two sheets of paper, letters, one formal looking and one on plain white paper. As the sheriff read the letters, Sandman returned with a box. He sat it on a small table on the porch.

When the sheriff finished reading, he said to his deputies. "You can leave. I have some things I need to say to Roger in private."

A curious look passed between the two men before they turned and went to the dark vehicle.

The sheriff's eyes dropped to the letters, and then he spoke to Roger. "Are you thinking of getting involved with this?"

"I am, and I wanted to let you know that. Where do you stand on this?"

He sighed. "When I was a new deputy, I saw some of this, but was too naïve and new to realize what was going on. Back then, I thought we could do no wrong, and learned it best not to question my higher-ups. Some questionable things were done in the old days."

"So, do you have any problems with me helpin' this woman and the group?"

"Roger, I believe in justice. If I didn't, I'd have quit years ago. If you and this group can prove this woman was wrongfully convicted, I won't stand in your way. As I said, things happened years ago that shouldn't have, but I warn you this. Some of the old school cops, lawyers, and judges that are still around may not want their past work reviewed. Also, this, everyone in prison says they're innocent. Few are. If you can filter out the few wheat kernels from all the chaff, have at it. Good luck. You'll need it."

"Thank you for that, sheriff. If you'd not approved, I'd have known I didn't want to work with you." Roger stopped to let his statement sink in. "Give me a day or so to look at what you have about this possible serial killer case."

"That's good with me. Now, I must go. Duty calls. Thank you, Roger. Let me know. I hope you take the case." He got up and left.

"Well, K9, let's see what information the sheriff has left. Hope it's good."

Chapter 2

Roger kicked back in his La-Z-Boy chair. He mulled over the papers the sheriff left. One reading would not be enough. Nothing jumped out at him, except the murder victims were all young women and dumped along I 95. The ones found in advanced decay provided little information other than they were dead. There were no cut marks on the bones or evidence of bullet trauma. When the hyoid bone had been located, it was undamaged and showed no sign of strangulation damage. A detailed search of the area provided no real additional information. A few old rusty bottle caps were all the CSI team recovered.

Coroner Will Corbett had examined all the bodies and done autopsies on the bodies intact enough to do autopsies on. Roger did a quick review of those files and put them aside for more careful reading later. This was where he usually checked to find good information and real clues. Only one curiosity had he found somewhat baffling. One corpse of the Jane Does seemed to be missing a large degree of her blood, and she was fresh enough that the coroner found fresh needle marks on her arms. The report said she had drugs in her system, but the toxicology report hadn't gotten back from the state lab. Rumor had it there was a large backlog, and it would just take time to get it back. The case could be as cold as the corpse when that happened.

Roger stroked his mustache as he pondered the information. He took another sip of beer. It was getting warm, so he chugged the remainder. "Ahh, beer, the elixir of life, that and coffee." He sat the empty can down.

"Grrrr." K9 came out from under Roger's old trailer. "Grrrr."

"What's up, girl? I don't see nothin'."

She looked toward the road. "Grrrr."

A truck came into view and stopped in front of Roger's place.

"Bill Kenney. Your favorite flatfoot. I should have known. Wonder what he wants? Probably be his same old usual PITA self. No biting, K9. You'll have to lick your butt to get the bad taste out of your mouth."

She growled again and went back under the trailer.

Canaveral Flats' one and only paid police officer, got out of his truck, opened and closed the gate without a curious donkey getting out. The little town was so broke it could hardly pay him. He proceeded down the sandy driveway to the trailer. When he got near, he hollered, "Hey, Roger, how's it hangin'?"

"What kind of a stupid greeting is that? How's it hangin'?"

Bill laughed. "I ran across it in a magazine in a doctor's office. Seems some women think that's how guys greet each other. Stupid, huh?"

"Very, and for the record, that's the first time anyone has ever said that to me, and I'd like you to make it the last, hombre. Understand?"

"No problem at all with that. The magazines you find in doctor's offices for women. One book tells you how to get slim and another is full of cake recipes."

"Why are you here, Bill? Couldn't find anyone else to annoy? State your business."

"Would you believe a wellness check on ole Roger and K9?"

"No."

9

"Didn't think so. How about I come looking for liquid refreshment?"

"Possibly, even probably, but I suspect there's more."

"You know me too well. Beer in the usual place? Get you one, too?"

"You know where they are, and yeah, get me one. I just finished off one and need another."

Bill went into the trailer and returned with two cans. "I see you're expanding your beer selection, Rolling Rock Pale Ale. Where did you get that? It's not distributed around here. Unique and tasty brew."

"I had a visitor. He knew I liked it and brought a 12 pack, that was only a 10 pack. He drank two on the way down from up north. It must have killed him to only drink two. I know he could have drunk at least half of them easily in one setting."

Bill popped the top and took a big sip. "Hey, that is smooth, refreshing."

"Give me my beer, you big galoot. If I know you, you'll suck 'em both down and give me none."

"Tis, tis. Grumpy old man. Here, take your beer."

"About time." Roger opened his and sipped it.

Bill said, "I will say this, grumpy old man, you're mellowing a little. You'd normally have called me a four-letter word, not a galoot."

Roger growled. "You're tempting fate. I may just bite you if K9 doesn't."

"How is K9?"

A growl came from under the trailer.

"Why, K9? How is the grumpy old man treating you?"

She growled again, louder.

Roger said, "You're pressin' your luck, old buddy. Did you come over to drink my beer, insult me, or something else?"

"Beer? Yes. Insults? As needed. And something else? Most definitely. I heard you got the I 95 Killer case, if you want it. How's it going?"

"How did you know about that?"

Bill said, "It was an open secret you were in consideration."

"So much for surprises."

"That and I ran into Hernandez at the Merritt Square Mall."

"What were you doing at the mall? You're not much of a mall shopper type guy."

"I took your cousin Suzie to a movie, and then we had a meal at the food court. She bought some plumbing supplies at Sears, too. Had another leak and she fixed it. How's your plumbing in this old fire trap holding up? She's quite a plumber handyman or handywoman whatever they call them these days. You could learn a few things from her."

Roger said flatly. "Guess she is. You still behavin' yourself around her?"

"Perfect gentleman. I told you. I don't mix business and pleasure. She's a good tenant. Keeps my efficiency up real nice and always pays the rent on time. Things are fine as they are, and I don't want to mess that up."

"What about Hernandez? Where did you see her?"

"She and Carlos were at the movie we went to see, *Harry and the Hendersons*. A guy on vacation with his family hits a Big Foot, and they take him home. It was kind of funny and corny. I didn't know they were there till the movie let out, and everyone headed for the food court."

"Wish I could have been there with them."

Bill said, "We sat at the same table. That boy of yours is growing like a weed. Smart, too."

"So, my name came up?"

"It did. Gloria was the one who confirmed to me you were gonna be offered the case. She put all the paperwork together and suggested you to the sheriff to head it up. She said she was already up to her eyeballs in work and knew if anyone could crack this case, it would be you."

"She did, did she? Well, I'll be."

"If there's anything more you need to know, it'll have to wait. I have to get back to work." He rose. "Thanks for the beer. Bye."

"I got more questions, but I guess I'll have to get the answers elsewhere. Bye."

Bill swiftly walked to his truck, and it soon disappeared down Canaveral Flats. Boulevard.

"Well, K9, we got through another Bill encounter without blood being shed."

She barked.

"Yeah, good for us. So, Hernandez has had her fingers all over this. Think I need to talk to her about this case, and more."

Chapter 3

Later That Same Day

"Wake up, sleepyhead. Quit sawing logs and talk to me."

Roger rolled his eyes and shook his head. **"Bill,** what brings you back so soon?"

"Thought we needed to talk."

"Oh please, not one of those talks. Not how I wanted to awaken from a pleasant dream. You'll never know how I hated to hear those words come out of my wife's mouth."

Bill gave Roger a knowing look. "Maybe I should have stated that better. I have some things I need to go over with a person I can trust." He stopped. "That better?"

"Yeah, that's better. So, what's on your mind? What's so important? Is it something to do with my cousin Suzy?"

"No, it has nothing to do with Suzy, but since you've mentioned her, she's doing fine."

Roger asked, "So, what does fine mean, really?"

"I've been a perfect gentleman with her, as I've said. We've had dinner a few times, even gone to a couple of movies together.

We both have our separate lives to live, but... Mostly, we just sit on the porch and talk."

"That's it?"

Bill said, "Yeah, that's it."

"Are you havin' feelings for her?"

Bill shifted in his chair, took a swig of beer, swallowed hard, and said, "Yeah, I think so. Never quite been there before. It was love 'em and leave 'em. Have some fun and move on. This is new ground for me."

"Does she know?"

"Of course she does. She's a woman. They can smell this stuff from a mile away."

Roger asked, "And she's good with it?"

Bill grinned. "She is. She knew I had feelings for her before I did."

Roger nodded. "That sounds about par for the course in the field of man-woman relationships."

"Roger, she's quite a woman. Been through a lot and like a Timex, took a licking and keeps on ticking."

"I think you know a lot more about her now than I do. She didn't talk too much about her past and life since we were children. I think her wounds were too fresh and still healing while she stayed with me and got herself back on her feet."

"That seems a good diagnosis, Doctor Roger."

"Easy with the doctor's title. I'm not an MD. I was a professor with a Ph.D."

"Okay, has your Suzie curiosity been satisfied?"

Roger said, "Yeah, now, what did you really come over here for?"

"You know I was working on the vote integrity in the county? Well, I found some things that frighten me."

"Must be serious to frighten you."

Bill said, "They are. I kept looking after I filed my report and found a lot more. I tried to report it, but the good ole boys and girls who run the county didn't want to hear it. They said, 'Let it go. It's over', but isn't that like ignoring a murder because the victim was already dead? Where's the justice in this matter?"

"Did it come across as a threat?"

"No, more like drop it and move on. Forget about it. We don't want to know any more."

Roger said, "I see."

"I remembered an incident several years ago. A fellow in Titusville tried to report a problem in the county government, and the officials went after him. It took everything he had to pay for lawyers to defend his innocence. In the end, he was broke and had his reputation ruined."

"I know what you're talkin' about. The process is the punishment. Powerful people can use the power of government and its deep pockets as a club to beat the little guy down kinda like David and Goliath, only David is unarmed."

Bill said, "I heard of another case down in Miami. Two brothers looking into vote fraud both died under mysterious circumstances."

"You worried?"

"A little. How about I tell you more and then you tell me if I need to worry?"

"Okay. I'm all ears."

Bill cleared his throat. "One party seemed to be benefiting more from the cheating, but both parties seemed to know it was going on."

"Why? That doesn't sound right."

"You don't get it. They're both in on it. One party runs the show, but makes sure the other party is taken care of. A lot of stuff is going on under the table."

"You mean like Harry Truman said, 'You have to be a crook to get rich in politics,'" Roger said.

"That's about it."

"So, what did you find that's so troubling?"

"Wide spread problems."

"Like?"

"Lots of phantom votes. Lots of names on the voter rolls with big red flags. Fake addresses, people dead for decades casting ballots, 60 people living in UPS boxes all with the same birthday, or RV park residents who moved decades ago, people voting from laundromats and other businesses, homeless who signed up decades ago, disappeared, but still vote from the shelter every election."

"That's it?"

Bill shook his head. "Far from it. Students voting from dorms that were torn down, people voting from streets that don't exist, 30 people casting votes from a one-bedroom apartment. Double votes and more, I'll spare you."

Roger whistled. "That's some heavy-duty stuff."

"It is. Think I have reason to be concerned?"

"I do."

They sat in silence for several moments.

Roger said, "Whatcha gonna do?"

"Watch my back more than usual. If you have any suggestions, let me know."

"I will. Let me think about it. As they say, two heads are better than one, even if one is a cabbage head."

Bill laughed. "Thanks. I needed that."

"Something will come up. Now, I need to pick your brain about two subjects. You're not on overload yet, are you?"

"Go ahead, if it's not as industrial strength as my problem."

Roger said, "Fortunately, it's not. As you know, I bought the old Flanagan property across the road and also the acreage on my west side. What should I do with them, if anything?"

"What have you got in mind? You thinking of getting rid of this old fire trap?" Bill asked.

"Maybe. I've thought about it, but it's serving me well. Kinda hate to get rid of it. It reminds me of when the family would come here when I was a kid."

Bill said, "Ah, sentimental attachment to this old tin can. Tell you this, I think you need to cut down that big gnarly oak tree that shades this place."

"Why? I'll lose my shade."

"It's got a big fork, and rot often gets in at that spot. And ants, too. They collapse in storms and even on still days. It would likely take out your trailer."

Roger said, "Yeah, I expect it could." He took a breath. "The lot next door's low and often has water on much of it. I'd have to bring in a lot of fill dirt to make it buildable, but as is, it makes good pasture for Donkey."

"True. How about the old Flanagan lot?"

"I was runnin' the possibility of puttin' a house on it. What do you think?"

Bill said, "Why not? You got the money. Get you out of this rattle trap tin can and into a real home. Why not? You already have water you can hook up and a septic system. You can thank Flanagan for that."

"Yeah, a house might be good. Stick build or a double wide?"

"Stick build would cost more and take longer. Be nicer, too, but it's up to you if you do decide to build at all."

Roger said, "Yeah, that was my conclusion."

"What was the other thing?"

"I'm bored. I got nuthin' to do, and I don't do well when I don't have a reason to get up. But I've been offered a case. Just don't know if I should take it."

"You have your son, Carlos."

"I do, but I need a real case I can sink my teeth in. I'm gettin' antsy. I need somethin' to do."

Bill said, "I have this feeling you'll get your wish. Something will turn up. Crime never takes a day off. I wish it did. Have patience."

"Patience? I want it now?"

Bill laughed. "Don't we all? Something is just around the corner." Bill glanced at his watch. "Holy smokes. I can't believe we've been talking so long."

"And we each only drank one beer. That's even more unbelievable."

"I got to get going."

Roger said, "What's so important?"

He lowered his head. "Suzie said we needed to talk."

"Not good. Good luck with that, ole buddy."

"Thanks, I think I'll need it. Bye."

"Bye."

Bill rushed off and his truck disappeared down the street. K9 emerged from under the trailer. "Hello, dog. What do you think of my possible plans for the properties?"

She smiled, turned her head, yawned, and barked.

"Yes, I'll see you, the cat, and Donkey are included in my plans. You guys are almost like family now. Which gives me an idea."

Chapter 4

Returning from town, Roger found himself behind Lester's truck. He followed him through Canaveral Flats to Lester's home. He pulled his truck up beside Lester's.

The old black man smiled. "Well, the things you see when you ain't got a gun. Actually, I do have a gun. I recognized it was you in that truck tailing me, but you passed the good guy test."

Roger grunted. "That's good to know."

"So, hello, Roger. What brings you here?"

"I need some advice and a sounding board."

"I can do that, but first, how about helping me get my groceries in the house and put away?"

Roger got out of his truck and said, "Sure, can't let the cold stuff get hot. Be happy to give you a hand. Find everything you needed at Publix?"

"I did. Today, you find full shelves with lots of selection. I remember back in WW II when everything was rationed and expensive and in short supply, if you could get it at all."

"Before my time, but I remember the stories my parents used to tell about the war and the Depression before it."

Lester said, "Hope to never see that again."

They took the groceries into Lester's old shotgun house and put the cold things away. The rest they left in the bags. Lester said he'd deal with it later.

"You want a brew?"

Roger said, "No, iced tea would be fine. Got any unsweetened?"

"How you ever gonna blend in as a Southern boy, not drinking super sweet tea?"

"Trying to watch my blood sugar and weight."

Lester laughed. "What about all that beer you drink? Don't you think dat gives you dat Dunlop's tire disease, too? You know, where your belly done lopped down over your belt."

Roger smiled. "One step at a time. Tea, please, unsweetened."

"Coming up."

Roger took a seat in an old overstuffed chair on the porch. Lester returned and handed Roger a tea. He sat in another chair that looked like the bottom had nearly fallen out.

"Thank you for the tea," Roger said. "Why don't you get a new chair? That one's falling apart."

"Just broke in. Fits my hiney perfectly."

"Guess it does." Roger took a sip. "How's your daughter? I haven't seen hide nor hair of her lately."

"Ruth's still living with me, but I don't see much of her. Seems she's busy, busy, busy. Working a job and doing all dat volunteer work. I told her she's burning the candle at both ends."

"Didn't do any good, did it?"

Lester said, "Nope, might as well been talking to a rock. She's a lot like me, even if we don't have any blood in common. Strong willed, determined, and a hard worker."

"Blood isn't everything that makes a family. She seems to have picked up a lot of your good traits."

Lester sighed. "And a few bad ones, too, but we won't go there." He took a sip and swallowed. "Now, what's on your mind? I know why you were wondering about Ruth. She speaks highly of you, but it seems you got something more on your mind. Spill the beans."

Roger rubbed his chin. "Yeah, I do. No foolin' you. I need some information. As you know, I bought some property around my place. The acreage on the east side I think I'm gonna leave as is. Donkey needs some more grass for grazing, but I was wondering what it would take if I wanted to build a house across the street at the old Flanagan place. It's got a water hook-up and a septic system already. It should be easy to run a new electric line from the pole. What kind of permits and inspections would I need?"

Lester slapped his knee. "None. This is Canaveral Flats. You're gonna live in it. Build it as safe as you want to live in it. If you build a firetrap and your place burns down, it's on you."

"Sounds like West Virginia." Roger took another sip. "Anything more?"

"I wouldn't build it at ground level. You need the floor level to be about two feet above the surrounding area. We get some hellacious rains from storms. I seen nine inches drop in three hours. Only time I heard of flash floods in this area. And then I seen over twenty inches fall in oh, two-three days during tropical storms and hurricanes. Build it strong. Them hurricanes can sure pack a punch with winds well over a hundred miles an hour for hours, even days."

"Know anybody who could do all that, starting with hauling in some dirt?"

"Sure do. I know a couple of guys from the Teamsters with their own trucks. One of them's between jobs and I'm sure he's looking to make some money on the side."

Roger said, "Good price, too?"

"Yeah, they'll do it for a friend of mine. You put up four corner stakes where you want the dirt dumped. They can level it out for you, too."

"Then let's do it."

"I'll send him around and you can work out the details."

"Do I need a contract or any money up front?"

Lester said, "A handshake will do. I trust you, and he trusts me. That will be all it takes." He shifted in his seat. "When you gonna do something about that old broken-down trailer you're living in?"

Roger said, "I kind of like it as is, but it is showin' signs of wear."

"That's the understatement of the day. I'm surprised it's made it this many years. It's seen a lot of storms and hurricanes. You need to consider replacing it, or are you gonna move into the new house?"

"I'm not sure at this time. Keepin' my options open."

They sat in silence for a moment.

Lester said, "What else is on your mind? I can tell there's more."

"You read me like a book." He paused. "I'm worried about Bill Kenney. He's openin' up a can of worms with his election and vote integrity probe. Some of the critters under the rocks he's overturnin' may not like it."

"I expect you're right. I told him as much. He talked with me about it. Definitely needs to be careful."

Roger nodded.

Lester said, "There's something more, isn't there?"

"Is it that obvious?"

"I know you too well."

Roger cleared his throat. "I got a letter from a woman in prison and her attorney. They say she's innocent and asked me to please look into her case."

"What's she in there for?"

"They say she burned down her house in Merritt Island with her kids in it ten years ago."

Lester nodded. "I remember it. Sad. So sad. But they all say they're innocent, don't they?"

"They do, but I saw some yellow and red flags when I read the paperwork on the case her attorney provided. I'm thinkin' about goin' to see her. She's incarcerated at the Central Florida Prison for Women this side of Orlando. Should I go or write it off as someone desperate to get out and will do anything to do just that?"

"It could be, but I think I'd go see her if you found something that would question the verdict of guilty."

Roger said, "I thought you may say that. What do I have to do in this state to visit her?"

"Pretty simple. Make an appointment and show 'em your official Canaveral Flats SOB badge at the gate."

Roger laughed. "SOB, Special Operations Branch. I'm a team of one." He paused. Think I'll ever see any pay for my work?"

"Not from Canaveral Flats. You've seen the houses in this town. Not much of a tax base for revenue."

Roger said, "So, that's it?"

"Yup, for law enforcement, attorneys, and family. You can call ahead and let them know you're coming, if you like."

Roger said, "Okay, I'll do that, soon. Thanks."

"Just keep me informed. After all, technically, as the Mayor of Canaveral Flats, I am your boss. I need to be in the loop."

"Will do."

A small fluffy puppy came around the corner of the house and ran up to Lester. She did a happy dance around his feet. "Good girl," he said, petted her head and stroked her back. "Good girl."

"Who's your new friend?"

Lester smiled. "This is Miss Happy."

"Don't look very old."

"Barely weaned. Her mother got out in the road, hit and killed, and the owner had to find homes for the pups quickly. I got Miss Happy or just Happy."

Roger said, "Yeah, she sure lives up to her name."

"Too young to know about all the problems in this world. She no pedigreed, just like most people. I think she's a Heinz 57 variety mutt."

"She a mixture alright." He shifted. "I guess you heard about the case I've been offered. I don't know whether to take it or not. Not sure what I'm gonna do."

Lester said, "Sounds like you got plenty to keep you busy without it. You could get busier. You could end up with a plateful and more than you can chew."

"I have a feeling there's something comin', foul winds, and it's about to hit the fan."

"Funny you mentioned it, but I do, too."

"I got to get goin'. Always good to talk with you, Lester."

"Maybe I should put out a sign like Lucy in Peanuts does, 'The Doctor is in. 5 cents.'"

"You'd get rich, but wouldn't have any spare time."

Lester said, "Maybe I won't. Just the same, always good to talk with you."

"Likewise. Got to be goin'. Bye."

"See y'all later."

Roger drove off and all the way home, couldn't shake an ominous feeling. Something or somethings were in the wind. He could almost taste it.

Chapter 5

Several days later

"Well, dog, I must be some better." Roger ran his hand across K9's head. "I no longer feel like something a bear pooped out and then fell over a cliff. Can't say I've felt that bad in years. Don't know what it was, but I'm glad it's over."

Being flat on his back for three days hadn't been any fun. The only time he'd gotten up was to run to the bathroom. He'd been going from both ends. Bill Kenney saw his newspapers piling up in the box and checked on him. Roger remembered telling him to go away. Yes, he was sick. No, he didn't want to go to a doctor. He'd treat himself with what was in the medicine cabinet. Bill said he looked sick enough to die. What if he did? He told Bill if it was his time to go, he should go away, and let him die in peace. See that his kid, Carlos, got everything if he croaked. And please feed the dog.

Bill shook his head and called him a stubborn ole galoot and a few other choice words, but did feed the dog and also checked on him when he could.

Roger made it through the night without having to get up for any reason. The eleven hours of sleep had done wonders for him. He almost felt human again. He stroked the dog's hairy head. "You're a good girl." She looked up with sympathetic eyes and licked his hand. "I'm not sure who rescued who, K9. I'm glad you're here, and that coyote didn't do you in. We owe a thanks to Donkey for taking care of that varmint."

K9 turned. "Gruff."

"Yeah, I see the truck. It's the mailman, mailperson, mailit, mailthingie, or whatever the Post Office is callin' them these days. Letter carrier is what I think they finally came up with. We'll let her move on before we go to the box. I image she's had enough unpleasant experiences with dogs in this neighborhood to last a lifetime."

The mail truck with the funny squared off corners stopped and made it's funny thunka-thunka engine sound.

"Dog, I don't know what keeps that thing runnin'. It sounds like the gum band's gonna break anytime, but it still keeps goin'." The thunka-thunka got louder and more rapid as it accelerated and disappeared down the road. It'd been a rough three days, but he now felt well enough to walk to the mailbox. "Let's go, K9."

She ran out the doggy door in the bottom of the porch screen door. Roger followed, but was in no hurry to get to the street. K9 waited for him at the gate. She tried to get through, but Roger shooed her back. "Behave yourself, girl. It's for your own good. Can't have you out runnin' loose in the road. Some crazy will come barrelin' along, and then you'll be flat. That would break my heart. You stay here."

She whined as he shut the gate. "Be a good girl. This won't take long. You know that."

He walked across the washboard sand street, got his mail, back across and opened the gate. K9 jumped up on him. "Now, what's got into you?" She sniffed at the mail. A doggy treat fell out, which she scarfed up, and it went down the hatch. "No wonder you look for the mailman."

As he neared the trailer, he heard the phone on the porch ring. He ran as fast as he could, considering his weakened state. "Hello," he panted.

"Roger, it's been a long time since I've heard you breathless like that."

He grimaced. "Gloria, what a surprise. How's the mother of my child today?"

"Pretty good. How about you?"

"Been sick for three days. First trip to the mailbox in as many days. I had to run to answer the call. Still feelin' like several cylinders are misfirin'. What's up?"

"Want to do lunch at Kelsey's?"

Roger thought for a moment. Lunch sounded good, but was his stomach up to it?

Gloria said, "It's on my dime."

"I had to consider if my belly was up for much solid food, but if you're buyin' and it's Kelseys, I'm game. How soon?"

"Around fifteen minutes. That too quick?"

"I can make it."

"Good. See you there, Roger."

The phone clicked. "Well, K9, looks like I've got a lunch date. Wonder what she wants? And she's buyin'. She's up to something." He rubbed his chin. "Maybe I'm being too suspicious, but maybe not. Guess I'll have to go see. You hold down the fort while I'm gone. And if Bill shows up, please don't bite him. You know what I told you about him."

She gave a little growl when she heard Bill's name.

"You **know** what I told you. Be good."

She barked, and Roger gave her a dirty look. "No bitin'."

She gave him a doggy smile and went under the trailer.

Fifteen minutes later, he pulled into the parking lot at Kelsey's. He'd worried he may not be up to the drive yet, but all went well, better than he expected. The lunch crowd hadn't arrived yet, and he found Gloria sitting at a table suitable for two.

"Roger, how was your ride?"

"I was worried my mouth had said yes, but my body would say no, but I made it intact."

"Good. I told the waitress I was expecting someone. I got water for both of us."

"I'm fine with that. My stomach needs a little babying today. Think I'll skip anything stronger."

He no more than sat down when the waitress appeared. Gloria knew what she wanted, and Roger ordered from memory.

Roger said, "You must have a special reason to want to see me, especially if you're paying the bill, but let me get the tip."

"That's fine," she said. "I've several reasons to ask you here. I hope you weren't too disappointed with the news. It's kind of bittersweet."

"What news?"

"I've been so sick the last three days. I haven't been anywhere or done nothin'. What news are you talkin' about?"

"Didn't the sheriff's department call you? Haven't you read the paper?" She asked.

"I didn't want to talk to anyone, so I put my answering machine in silent mode. I saw it flashin', and I haven't had time to see if there's anything important. Probably just sales pitches. Buy this. Buy that. You know."

"You haven't looked at the newspaper?"

"Nope. They're still wrapped in the plastic sheath they came in. What's the big deal I don't know about?"

Her eyes widened. "Your big case has been solved. The one the sheriff came to see you about."

"Bill told me that you suggested me, but what do you mean it's been solved?"

"Yeah, I recommended you for the case? Me, Gloria. We've been so busy, and I knew a fresh set of eyes from someone as qualified as you could figure it out. And yes, we believe it's been solved. Four days ago, a naked woman barely alive pounded on a door in Malabar down in the south end of the county. The woman who was renting the house was afraid to open the door, so she called 911. The cops came, and the woman told them a tale they could barely believe. She'd been drugged, abducted, tied to a table, raped, and had a man stick an IV in her arm, and drink her blood. She barely had enough left in her to be alive. He left, and she managed to escape. The man, who works for a company doing defense work, has been arrested.

"A search of his house turned up all kinds of evidence that linked him to the series of unsolved murders you were asked about investigating. He's confessed to harming the woman and one more, but after talking to a lawyer, he's gotten tight lipped. I think he's working on a plea deal. If he fesses up to all he's done, the prosecution could possibly take the death penalty off the table. So there's a 99% chance your case is solved. And don't expect a thank you for your help from the sheriff."

Roger said, "Well I'll be." He shook his head. "I'm dumbfounded. I don't know if I should be happy or disappointed, probably a little of both. This news is a shock to my fragile, recovering system. Gonna take a while to digest this."

"I see our food coming. You can digest the two together, and then I have another thing to talk to you about."

"Carlos?"

She nodded.

"I thought so."

The waitress dropped off their food. They leisurely ate it and made small talk between bites. When they were done, Roger wiped his mouth. "That was good, especially since you're payin' for it. Now, what about our son, Carlos?"

"Yes, it was good." She paused. "Carlos. He's been asking a lot about you. Some stuff I know. Some I don't. He wants to be more in your life. I want you to be more in his life. A kid needs a dad. God knows I can try my best, and God knows single moms do their best, but you're available and want to be in this picture. As I see it, we have two options. He can spend more time with you, or you can spend more time at my place. I can give you a key. It could be more convenient that way. You know the crazy hours cops work."

Roger said nothing.

"Do you need to think about it?"

"Yes, and no. I have no problem with spendin' more time with him or him spendin' more time at my place. I'm just not sure I want a carte blanche invite to your place. Let me consider that."

"Fair enough."

Roger said, "Now I have to figure what to do with myself. I'd just gotten used to the idea of a new case. I finally decided to take it, and then, just like that, the rug's been pulled out from under me. Now what?"

Gloria said, "Oh, I'm sure something will come up. Surprises are always on the horizon. That's a guarantee."

"Do you know something I don't?"

"Maybe."

"And you're not at liberty to say."

"I'd have to kill you if I did."

"Thought you might say something like that. Okay, I can wait. Keep me in suspense." He smiled.

She smiled back. "Yes, that's the way it has to be for now." She looked at her watch. "My, but time flies when you're having fun. You go ahead. Looks like there's a line at the cash register."

"I'll do that. Thanks for lunch, and I'll consider what you said."

"See you, Roger."

"Bye."

Roger bypassed the line at the door and walked out. After all, Gloria was paying. Traffic was light on US 1. Canaveral Flats Boulevard was as rutted as ever. He waved to Fred as he passed Miller's Store. He thought he saw the autistic man give a half-hearted wave back. It was better than he expected. He stopped at the gate in front of his trailer, opened it, closed it before Donkey could get out, and drove down to the trailer. The day had been full of unexpected surprises.

Wonder what surprises tomorrow will bring?

Chapter 6

Bright and early the next day, a noisy, large dump truck woke Roger from a sound sleep in his La-Z-Boy chair on his porch. Well, actually, it woke K9 who woke Roger. She made a big fuss.

"Quiet, girl. I've been expectin' him."

Roger stroked her head, got up, gave her some dog food, and headed out the door to the road.

"Guard the fort while I'm gone, K9."

She paid him no mind as she gulped the food from her bowl. Soon, Roger was talking with the driver in the Schultz Trucking vehicle. He got out, and Roger showed him where he wanted the dirt on the old Flanagan lot placed. After a brief conversation about the price, they shook hands. A deal had been struck.

An hour later, the truck returned as Roger finished his breakfast and dumped the first load of fill dirt. This went on for the rest of the day until dark. The driver said he'd be back tomorrow to level it out and pack it down.

During the day, Roger read a book by Tony Hillerman about cops and crime on the big Navajo Reservation in Arizona. One of the librarians, Rick, at the Port St. John Library, not Connie, who had the hots for Roger and anything that wore pants, suggested the author, and Roger was glad he had.

Around noon, the Shaman showed up. As usual, he appeared like a phantom.

"Hello, white man."

Roger jumped. "Would you just walk up the driveway, so I can see you comin'?"

He thought he saw a slight grin on the Indian's face. "What fun that?"

"You liked to scared me out of a month's growth." Now he was sure he saw a grin on the other man's face. "So, what brings you to my humble abode today? More warnings of impending disaster? What is it today? Seems like whenever you show up, my life gets very interesting. That orchid you gave me a while back caused a lot of trouble, and that's just one of the many things you—"

"Sorry."

"That's all you can say?"

The Shaman sat quietly for a moment. "Very sorry."

Roger was sure the other man was grinning, though he tried not to show it. Roger grunted. "So, what is it this time?"

"It time."

"It time? It time for what?"

The Shaman said, "**You know**. It time you tell the story of the Ancient Ones in the pond. They speak. Say now the time."

"Why? Why now and not tomorrow or a month from now?"

"They say now the time. Not say why now, but now the time."

Roger said, "I want to know why now."

The Shaman shrugged his shoulders, "Just messenger. Not know. You ask them. They tell you, maybe."

Roger thought about what he said.

"Ancient Ones not like you or me. Reason different. From different time. I not understand either, but now the time."

They sat in silence for some time before Roger spoke. "The last time you were here, you spoke of danger and impending doom for me."

Shaman nodded.

"Well?"

"Well, what?"

"Has it passed? Have things changed?"

The Shaman was silent for some time. "Shaman not know." He paused. "Unusual. Most unusual."

Roger said, "That was certainly not helpful."

"No."

Roger studied the Shaman's face, but he couldn't read it. It remained a blank page. He said nothing more. Roger waited for the Shaman to speak, but he remained silent, staring off to the horizon. A minute or more passed when the Shaman turned to Roger. "Must go. It time. The Ancient Ones say so."

"That's it?"

"Danger, Roger Pyles. Must be careful." He exited the porch and disappeared into the nearby marsh.

K9 came out from under the trailer.

"Well, there you are, my protector. Some protector you are. You didn't tell me he was comin' or rush to my defense when he got here." She wagged her tail. "Though I doubt if I needed defending. He could have had me for sure, if he'd wanted. What do you think he meant by danger and being careful?"

She barked.

"I thought that's what you'd say. You're as clueless as I am."

A rumble at the road told them a large truck was approaching. It dumped another load of dirt across the street on the lot. The driver waved as he left. Roger returned the wave. "You know, K9, the Shaman has a way of knowin' when someone's comin' and makin' himself scarce, but I think I better watch my back, and I want you to do the same."

She barked.

"Good girl. This could go western real quick."

Chapter 7

"Ruff."

Roger stirred in his La-Z-Boy chair and stretched. "K9, you just interrupted a pleasant dream. What is it? Can't be that rascal Bill Kenney, or you'd be growlin'. What is it?"

"Ruff."

Motion caught Roger's eye. Pastor Nassey was walking down the driveway. "No wonder you weren't makin' a commotion."

K9 gave him a doggy smile and yawned.

"Hey, Roger, permission to come on board."

"You know the welcome mat's always out for you, Pastor. And for your information, it's aboard, not on board."

The Pastor laughed. "Sorry, not much of a sailor." He stopped. "I saw Gloria Hernandez at the gas station. She said you'd been sick, so I thought I'd better check before I made myself at home. Didn't know if you were up for uninvited visitors."

"I'm doin' better. It'll be a cold day in hell when you're not welcome here, Pastor."

"Still thought it would be better if I checked first."

"Come on down," Roger hollered in his best *Price is Right* voice.

A few, short moments later, Pastor opened the screen door on the porch and entered. K9 greeted him, and he rubbed her head. "Good girl. You keeping Roger out of trouble?" He took a seat.

Roger said, "She's doin' her best. Be glad she likes you. She usually growls at Bill Kenney. Never has liked him."

"Bill's been known to rub some people the wrong way. And animals, too."

"Yup, that's Bill for you. Not sure if it's his charming personality or the fact he's a cop."

Pastor said, "I think it's a little of both."

"Believe you could be right. So, what brings you to my humble abode today?"

"Home visitation day with the sick and elderly."

Roger interrupted. "Which one am I?"

"Well, you're not old, Roger, but you can be a sick puppy."

"K9, you gonna let him insult me like that?"

She barked.

Roger said, "See, she's not havin' it."

Pastor smiled. "Can't argue with her." He paused. "You see, Mrs. Tallman's not doing well. Seems the cancer's come back with a vengeance after years of remission. She could go at any time. A week to two months at best. She's going downhill fast."

41

Roger's mind drifted off. Tallman. There's a name he hadn't heard lately, and he wished he hadn't heard it now.

"I'm sorry to hear that, Pastor."

"I know you worked the Cowboy Gene bank robbery case and found out her youngest daughter, Peggy Sue, was the thief. Do you feel responsible for Peggy Sue'e death?"

Roger hesitated. "No, Pastor. She made her choices and had to live with the consequences."

Pastor nodded. "Sounds like what the Good Book teaches. Whatever we sow, we also reap whether in this life or in the next."

"Did Gloria tell you the big serial killer case I was all gearin' up for has been solved?"

"No, but I did read something in the newspaper about the one I believe you're referring to."

"Yeah, they're also 100% sure they got their man. I've been told to stand down. I was all hepped up and gungho to go at it full-steam, and now I have no case to work. It's disappointin' and kind of sad. Don't get me wrong. I'm glad they got the guy, and he can do no more harm, but it's like they pulled the rug out from under me. I know what a ship without a rudder feels like."

"I'm sure something will come up to keep you busy. Crime never seems to take a day off." He paused. "It's funny you mention that feeling. I had lunch with an acquaintance who happens to be an atheist. He always tries to trip me up on my Christian beliefs."

"Does that bother you?" asked Roger

"At one time it did, but as I've grown in my faith, I welcome the challenge. As the Bible says, as iron sharpens iron, so one man sharpens another man's wits."

"Sounds interesting. Tell me more, Pastor."

"I try to use times like this as a teaching experience. My goal isn't to whack him over the head with Biblical truths, but to put a stone in his shoe, make him uncomfortable, and get him to think. He said people are only Christians because they seek meaning in life. He said we're desperate for meaning and fear the unknown of what happens after we die.

"I told him he was right in one aspect. My faith does give my life ultimate meaning, value, and purpose, but that's not my only reason to believe. You see, these virtues are impossible without God. If there is no God, then no ultimate meaning, value, or purpose can exist. We're just cosmic accidents with none of those things and destined to total annihilation and extinction when our sun burns out. It's not a problem for me as a Christian, but for you, an atheist, since you're admitting my belief in God gives me all of those. Does your atheist's beliefs do that? You see, without God, your life has none of those qualities."

Pastor laughed. "He was surprised. He stammered he'd have to think about that. I said that was fine. Roger, very seldom are people open to the ideas that their lives are totally meaningless and without purpose. I believe God is the only solution to this problem."

Roger said, "I think I know where you're comin' from. As you know, I was a college professor. Because of the influence of my late wife, Kay, I took a step back and began to observe the people around me, teachers and students. They were lookin' for meaning and tryin' to fill it with all kinds of hedonistic and permissive philosophy. It seemed to make them happy on the surface, but if you went an inch deep, it was all an illusion. They had no commitment to worthy goals. They lacked an anchor to hold them in place when they needed it."

He continued. "The scientists I knew, when they'd get buck naked honest, would quietly admit how impossible evolution was for explaining how life and everything we see began. It had no answer to where life came from. It was one of the things that got me on my quest for answers."

Pastor said, "I think you know my answer to those questions."

Roger nodded, "But you're gonna tell me, anyway, right?"

Pastor smiled. "You know me too well, so here goes." He cleared his throat. "The Psalmist says we're fearfully and wonderfully made. That means we're special and awesome. Our bodies have billions of cells and a myriad of parts that all have to work together just so. I believe God crafted each of us with His own hands. He uniquely made us all. We are His handiwork. I can just see the angels watching in amazement as He worked and hollering, 'Wow! Way to go, God! Good job!'"

Roger said, "Yeah, I gotta agree. This world just has too much order for it to have randomly, haphazardly happened."

"All creation speaks and testifies of its Creator." Pastor said, "After that sermonette, I feel like passing a plate."

Roger said, "Look around. Does this look like a place where you'll get a full offerin' plate?"

They laughed.

Pastor said, "Everyone comes into this world with nothing and leaves with nothing no matter how rich or poor they are while on this sojourn." He glanced at his watch. "Mercy, how time flies when you're having fun. I have another shut-in to visit. Fortunately, it's just around the corner. Any more discussion will have to wait for later."

Roger smiled. "That's quite alright. You've left me with more than enough to think about. Get goin' to your visitation. It's always good when you stop in. I always feel uplifted from your visit. Some other people, well, I'm happy when they leave."

Pastor laughed. "Please, don't mention any names. And Roger..."

"Yes?"

"I'm sure something will come up to keep you busy."

"I expect you're right on that. You better get goin'."

Pastor nodded. "Till next time. Take care."

"Thanks. You, too."

Pastor's car soon disappeared down Canaveral Flats Boulevard.

Roger's eyes drifted off to the horizon. *Peggy Sue Tallman. Was she really dead? Had he done the right thing letting her go down in Baja, Mexico?*

He shifted in his chair, reached over, and stroked K9's head. "Well, dog, he sure left me with a headful of stuff. And I think he's right about something comin' up to get my attention. Just wonder what it is."

K9 barked, and Roger smiled. "Thought you'd say that."

Chapter 8

The next morning, Roger was feeding his critters when Schultz's big dump truck pulled up the road in front of his trailer. It had a front-end loader on a trailer behind it. He waved at the driver, who waved back. Quickly, the workman removed the chains that secured the machine on the trailer. He drove it off the back, through the open gate, and started to level out the dirt piles dumped the day before.

Roger was finishing his breakfast when he saw the workman coming down his driveway, and he had a concerned look on his face. K9 barked at him. "He's a friendly, girl, though he doesn't look too happy right now. Wonder what's up. Guess we'll find out soon."

"Mr. Pyles, hope you are well today. I think we may have a problem. Before I went any further, I wanted to talk with you."

"Just call me Roger. Mr. Pyles seems too formal. What's the problem, Ronald?"

"I found the gate open this morning. Did you open it?"

"No, I thought you left it open. Just forgot after you were done."

"I closed the gate before I left yesterday afternoon about dusk. Someone's been on the property overnight. Did you notice anything?"

Roger said, "Can't say I did. When it's warm, I like to sleep on the screened porch, but it was cool last night, so I slept inside. K9 was with me. She kept tryin' to crawl in bed with me, but I shooed her to her doggy bed. Guess she thought it was a one dog night type of cold."

"Well, someone's been there, and I think they left something."

"Tell me more."

Ronald cleared his throat. "I was leveling off the fill dirt. I started in the front and was working my way toward the back. When I got there, I saw the fill dirt had been disturbed."

"Disturbed? How so?"

"I think someone buried something there about the size of a large suitcase or duffle bag. I didn't like the looks of it, so I stopped and came over here to tell you."

Roger said, "You did the right thing. Hard to tell what they left, but all kinds of red flags are poppin' up in my brain."

"That was my feeling, too. Something just didn't smell right."

"I'll get a rod and a shovel. The rod will sink through the soft dirt. If and when we hit something, we can find out what they left."

Ronald said, "I've got a shovel in the truck. I'll get it, and we can both dig if need be."

"Sounds like a plan."

Roger got the rod and shovel from the shed/stable Donkey called home. Donkey wanted attention, as usual. Roger stroked his big head and neck. "Good boy. Glad you've been stayin' out of trouble. Guess you like the extra area to roam. More grass should make you happy." Donkey cooed and nudged Roger on the side. "I can't hide nothing from you, can I?" Donkey cooed with more enthusiasm. "Here you go, buddy, one apple I was savin' for later." Donkey took the apple in his lips, chewed a little, and swallowed it down. His eyes begged for more. "That's all. I got no more. Move along. I have work to do." His eyes grew sadder. "No, that's all there is. Munch on some grass. I have things to do." Donkey got the idea and sauntered off. He did turn his head to see if Roger had changed his mind. "Go. Don't make a pest of yourself." Donkey strolled off. Roger walked to the road with K9 next to him.

Ronald was waiting. "Ready?"

"Yeah. Show me what you found. Let's walk on the leveled dirt. If this is something bad, we don't want to disturb anything more."

"Gotcha."

The uncompacted fill dirt sank below their feet as they walked to the rear.

"There," Ronald said. "Looked to me like someone hastily tried to cover up something. If they'd taken a little more time, I might have missed it."

"Yeah, I see what you're sayin'. Let me check things out. The less disturbance, the better. I've had some experience with matters like this. And stay off that area you used as a roadway back. There could be some tire tracks that could be evidence if this does turn out bad."

Ronald nodded. "Anything I can do?"

"Sit tight for now."

Roger eased his way to the disturbed earth. K9 went around him and sniffed at the dirt. Her face twisted, and she sneezed. "K9, get outta here. Don't need you messin' around." He picked her up and handed her to Ronald. "Hold her by the collar. Don't need her contaminating whatever we have here."

"Okay."

Roger poked in the fill dirt with the rod. In some places, it sank in, hitting nothing, but the rod stopped about a foot or so down. He continued until he could see a pattern. "Yeah, it does seem about the size of a suitcase. Give me the shovel."

Ronald handed it to him, and he began to dig. It didn't take long to uncover a hard sided Samsonite piece of luggage, definitely not carry-on size, but checked. Roger uncovered the top. K9 sniffed the air and sneezed.

"Not good," Roger said. "I've got a bad feeling about this."

He found the latches. They weren't locked, undid them, opened the lid, and took a look. "Oh, no." He quickly shut the lid.

Ronald asked, "Bad is it?"

"Yep. We have a body. Time to get the police involved."

"Aren't you the police?"

"I am, but I'm also a witness now involved in a possible crime scene. We need someone else. I'll contact Bill Kenney and he can take it from there."

Ronald said, "You know better than me."

Roger said, "You need to stick around. The forensics people will have a bunch of questions for you and me both. It could be a long day."

"I was afraid of that."

"You may want to find something else to do for a few days. The crime scene guys could have this restricted for several days."

Ronald, "Yeah, I thought so."

Roger said, "Now the hard part begins. Who is she? How did she die? Who put her here, and why?"

"This isn't how I wanted my day to start."

"Me neither, and I think it will only get worse."

Chapter 9

To say the least, things got rather crazy after the discovery of the body. Chief of Police Bill Kenney rushed over after getting the phone call from Roger, who showed him what he'd found. They were careful not to further disturb the crime scene. Bill called the Brevard County Sheriff's Department.

Bill and Roger secured the area with crime scene tape and locked the gate at the old Flanagan place. A Crime Investigation Scene crew showed up within the hour and went right to work. One officer questioned Ronald and Roger about how they'd found the body and what they'd done before calling the police. He took notes on a legal pad. A female officer found some tire tracks, probably from the vehicle that dropped her here, and got a good mold of them. She made some molds of footprints, too, that weren't Ronald or Roger's. They were as big as Roger's but much wider.

The coroner, Will Corbett, showed up a little later. He checked the body and did a quick investigation. A more thorough one would have to wait until he got her back to the morgue. He walked over to Roger's trailer. Ronald and Roger sat on the porch with K9.

"This is not how I wanted to see you, Roger," Will said. "And is this Ronald, the man who found the body?"

Before Roger could respond, Ronald said, "I discovered something was not as it should be. I showed the disturbed earth to him, and he uncovered the suitcase, opened it, and found her."

"Is that how it was, Roger?"

"Yup, pretty much so. Not how I expected to start the day, either. I noticed bruises on her neck. Do you think she was strangled?"

Will said, "There's a strong possibility she was. I'll know more when I can do a thorough exam."

Roger asked, "Any idea when she was killed?"

"I'm not sure we have a murder, but I expect we do. I've been surprised before. I do know she wasn't killed here, and I believe she died sometime yesterday. Got a lot of things to consider. The cool weather. Buried in a suitcase under a foot of earth. Yesterday's an educated guess. Again, I need to do some more calculations to give as accurate as possible answer to that important question. Roger, I have your phone number, but I need Ronald's."

"Okay," Ronald said. He read off ten numbers. "Now, can I go? I need to make some money today. Baby needs a new pair of shoes."

Will said, "I don't think you're needed here. Believe we have it covered. You may want to ask the CSI team to be certain."

"I'll do that." He exited the porch and walked to the other side of the road where his dump truck was parked.

Will glanced at Roger. "Now, we can talk."

"I thought you were waitin' for him to leave."

"Certain things he didn't need to know." He stopped. "Yeah, I think she was murdered. I've yet to hear of a naked, attractive female hurriedly buried in a suitcase that wasn't murdered. The marks on her neck were probably from some big powerful hands, and she had more marks on her arms and legs, like she'd been bound. That all says murder to me."

"Me, too."

"Sure would be nice if we knew when she was buried there."

Roger rubbed his chin. "Had to be last night. Got anything more to say?"

"Not at this time. I know how to reach you if needed. I'll take the body to town and see what more I can find."

"Hey, I just had a thought. Take me to Miller's Store. I'll walk back."

Will said, "Why? You need some chips?"

"Yeah, I do, but I might know someone who can help us out with this case."

"Who?"

"Fred."

"Fred who?"

"Mrs. Miller's son."

"That strange guy who helps at the store?"

"That's the one."

Will looked dumbfounded.

"Trust me," Roger said. "Guy's a lot sharper than he looks."

They walked to the van with the body in the back, and Will drove to the store. There were no cars parked in front of the building, and Fred sat on a bench out front. They got out, but Fred just stared ahead.

"Hello, Fred," Roger said. "How's life treatin' you today?"

"Better than some people. Been a lot of cops around. Cops have a way of showing up when something bad happens."

"Something bad did happen."

"Who's your friend?"

"This is Will. I'll vouch for him."

Fred said nothing, but Roger could tell he understood. "Fred, you still havin' trouble sleepin'?"

"We are. Thanks for asking. We took melatonin for a while, but it did no good. Still can't sleep through the night. Mom neither. Sometimes we sit on the porch here, talk, and watch the world go by, but it's usually pretty quiet around here after midnight. Bugs get a little hungry, but not so much with this cooler weather."

"Were you on the porch last night?"

"Yes. We sat over on the side. Dark there. Light from the night light doesn't reach there and fewer bugs. More secluded there."

"Much traffic last night?"

"It was dead, except for one car, a Chevy Impala, fairly new, a 1984 model. Came in slow like he wasn't sure where he was going, and then left several hours later in a big hurry."

"Did he see you?"

Fred said, "No."

"You sure it was a he?"

"Yeah, big man."

"Thank you, Fred."

"Want the license number? It was an out-of-state tag."

Roger smiled. "Sure, what is it?"

Fred gave him the seven letters and numbers on the New York license plate. "Need any groceries? Got a sale on strawberries. Grown over in Plant City. Really ripe and good."

"Maybe later, Fred. I got to get back to my place. Thanks."

"You're welcome."

They got in the truck and headed back to Roger's old trailer.

"Amazing," Will said. "Absolutely amazing."

"I know. Fred has either Asperger's or he's autistic or both, and he's a savant, a wizard with numbers."

"I'll drop you off and tell the CSI team what we found out."

"Sounds good to me. You ready for another adventure like the road trip we took to Key West?"

"I don't know. It was fun, and as you say, an adventure I will never forget, but we nearly got killed. I didn't sign up for hazardous duty."

Roger smiled. "Yeah, life can be like that. You let me know if you want to do it again."

"I'll have to think on that. Working with the dead also has certain advantages. I've never had a corpse try to kill me. And if one does rise up off the table, I'm outta there, and won't stop running until I'm in Daytona."

"I'll take that as a maybe."

"Whatever," Will said. "We're here. Now, get out and leave me with the non-threatening corpse. Being around you can be dangerous to one's health."

Roger laughed. "Till next time."

He got out and walked to his trailer. Will passed the information to the team still working at the potential crime scene and then left with his quiet passenger. It wasn't even noon, and Roger already felt like he'd put in a full day. His stomach growled. Lunch time would be soon. Wonder what Gloria Hernandez, mother of his child, was doing?

Chapter 10

"Hello."

"Gloria, how's it goin'? I called the office, and they said you took the day off. Are you okay?"

"More or less, thou thrasonical, logger-headed rampallian, also known as Roger Pyles. I was feeling a little off when I got up this morning, so I did something I rarely do, took a sick day."

"And you're reading Shakespeare, it would seem."

"Yes, thou braggart, dullard, and scoundrel."

"Yup, definitely Shakespeare. No one else insults like that. What's up?"

"Just a bad day. I think the job's getting to me. Dealing with crime and suffering day after day can be a downer, and today was one of those days."

Roger said, "I know about feeling down. Sounds like you need some cheering up. I could get a carry out and stop over. We need to have a Carlos discussion, among other things. You feeling well enough for that?"

"I think so. What did you have in mind?"

"Chicken from Publix with some sides?"

"Sounds good."

Roger said, "Give me 45 minutes to an hour."

"That works fine. Would you like wine with that?"

"Sure."

"A friend who works for Customs gave me a bottle of something they confiscated at the Port."

Roger laughed. "Nothing like seized wine to make a meal. I'll see you ASAP."

"Okay. See you soon. Bye."

Traffic was light on the way over to Merritt Island, but an accident on North Courteney slowed him down. He picked up the meal at the supermarket and headed for Gloria's apartment. He raised his hand to rap on the door when it opened. His eyes grew wide with surprise.

Gloria laughed. "I heard you coming, and I'm hungry. Getting my appetite back. Come on in. I've got the table ready."

Roger went in, and they were soon eating. He said, "Love Publix's chicken. Just the right amount of spices. The wine's good, too. Taste like something I had before, but I can't place it. What is it?"

"Don't know. The label was missing. That's the reason they confiscated it."

"And I see they disposed of it properly."

Gloria said, "Don't tell anybody."

Roger laughed. "I know how the system works. No need to remind me."

She laughed, too. "Yeah, who watches the watchers? It is pretty good wine."

"Tastes expensive."

"Yeah, my friend said the man whined up a storm when he took it away."

They finished eating. Roger asked to have his glass refilled. Gloria topped off her glass, too.

She said, "So, what did you want to talk about?"

"I'm havin' a house built on the property I own across from my old trailer."

"You going to move in?"

"Probably not. I'm happy where I am."

She said, "You really need to upgrade out of that old firetrap. Our son needs a father."

"You're not the first one to tell me to get rid of it. Guess I'll need to in time." He paused. "You know, I thought maybe you might be interested in it. You said it would be nice to be out of an apartment. Have a yard you could call your own, and you also told me that I should spend more time with Carlos. That would be a way we could do that."

Gloria was silent for a moment. "I don't know. This is quite a surprise. I'm going to have to think about it." She stopped. "How's the wine?"

"Tasty, and maybe a little strong. I can feel a little buzz."

"Me, too. Want some more?"

"Sure, why not? I don't need to be anywhere."

She filled their glasses with the wine that remained in the bottle, and they drank freely.

She gave Roger a silly grin. "You think we could ever be an item, you know, like we were in Vegas and beyond?"

"I don't know. We sure had some fun at that convention in Vegas and wondered about the other."

She gave him a kiss and looked into his eyes. "Did you like that?"

He smiled.

"Would you like another?"

He nodded, but before she could kiss him, he kissed her deeply, and soon their arms wrapped around each other. Clothes flew everywhere and two inebriated naked people found their way to Gloria's bedroom.

**

Three hours later

Gloria awoke with a start. "What was that?"

"Huh?" stumbled out of Roger's sleepy mouth.

"Mom, I'm home."

Gloria swore. "Carlos is home from school! What will we do?"

"Mom?" He saw the clothes on the floor and went to his mother's bedroom. "Mom?" He saw them in bed together. "I'll be in my room, Mom." Carlos left and they could hear the door to his room closing.

"Now, what do we do?" Gloria said.

Roger said, "Get dressed?"

She said, "I'll retrieve our clothes." She slid out of bed and grabbed a bathrobe to cover herself, then went into the living room and gathered their attire scattered all over the room. After dropping it on the bed, she said, "Hurry, get dressed."

"Okay, but it's a little late now." He hopped out of bed and put his underwear on.

"You're telling me." Hastily, they covered themselves up and sat on the bed.

"Roger, if you thought I invited you over for this, you're wrong. I didn't plan it. It just happened."

"No, I don't believe you did. You'd have showed me out before Carlos got home." He stopped. "I thought that wine tasted familiar. I've had something like that before. It was a sherry or brandy, probably 20% alcohol or more. No wonder we lost our inhibitions."

"I wasn't trying to seduce you, use sex to get you wrapped around my finger."

Roger said, "No, I don't believe you did. I may be a man, but I'm smarter than that. Just the same, it was very enjoyable. One thing we are is good in bed."

"Yeah, we are, but that's not enough to base a relationship or marriage on."

"Very true."

"Now, what do we tell Carlos?"

Roger said, "Well, he's no dummy. He knows what was goin' on. How about we tell him it's a complicated adult situation we're workin' on?"

"I don't think that will be sufficient."

"I'll work on it."

"You ready to go face the music?"

Roger sighed. "Guess so."

They rose from the bed, and Roger found a seat in the living room. Gloria went to Carlos' door. "Carlos, could you come out? We need to talk."

She heard a muffled, "Okay, Mom," through the door. She sat in a chair across from Roger.

Carlos came out and took a seat in his favorite chair. He looked at them innocently. "What did you want?"

Gloria said, "We ah... we wanted to say that...well... you see..."

Roger said, "What your mother's tryin' to say is that we're attempting to work out our relationship, and it's complicated in an adult kinda way."

She said, "Yeah, with adults, it can get complicated."

Carlos was quiet for a moment. "Okay, can I go back to playing Nintendo? I was having a great time with Mario."

"Sure, have fun. Run up a big score."

"Will do, Mom." He got up and went to his room. The door closed, and they could hear various sounds coming from the Nintendo game.

Roger said, "Well, that went better than expected."

"He's a smart kid. He knows what's going on. He'll be nine in a week, but he's going on twelve or thirteen in some ways. Give it a few days, and he'll have something more to say about today."

"So, what are we goin' to do, Gloria? This is complicated."

"Tell me about it. I guess we just keep puttering along until we reach some kind of a conclusion."

"Yeah, I think so. And I wanted you to know, if you did take up my offer to move into the house I'm havin' built, it's because I want to be near Carlos. I'm not doing it and expecting conjugal relations as part of the bargain. What happened today just happened."

She said, "Yes, sex can mess with our minds. It already has."

Roger nodded. "You think about it. It's months in the future before the house will be done."

"I'll do that."

"I better be goin'. There's a situation out there I need to check on. Seems someone buried a murdered woman on the property in the fill dirt I had delivered."

"What?" She stopped. "Are you serious?"

He nodded. "Serious as a heart attack."

"Roger, you're full of surprises, pleasant and unpleasant."

"You, too, Gloria. I better be goin'. And I don't need a kiss goodbye. I think we did enough of that today."

"Guess so. Call me when you need to."

"I will." He got up, went to the door, said bye, and left.

"Bye," she hollered after him.

He got in his truck. A glance told him Gloria was looking down from her window. He waved as he left, and she waved back. He pulled out on Courtenay Parkway and sighed. He wasn't sure how this would work out, but it definitely had gotten more complicated. That he was sure of.

Chapter 11

Roger thought about what had just happened as he drove. There always would be that animal magnetism when it came to Gloria, but he wasn't sure he liked where it seemed to go. He felt a little numb from the alcohol, but he'd driven in far worse shape in his younger days. He didn't feel like he was over the legal limit, but he knew he was close, so he drove just under the speed limit and very carefully.

Gloria and alcohol were a bad combination. He'd try not to do that again. He wondered what she was thinking about their rendezvous and how she'd explain it to Carlos. She was a sexy little devil when she wanted to be. He grinned. Most women are when they want to be.

Traffic on US 1 was heavy, and he had to slow down to a crawl in several school zones. He couldn't think of anything he needed at the grocery store, so he turned on Canaveral Flats Boulevard. The paved section soon ran out, and he bounced along on the washboard road to his house. The CSI team seem to be wrapping it up. He no more than sat in his La-Z-Boy chair when he saw a county deputy walking down his driveway. Deputy Yates was about to pay him a visit.

"Hey, Roger. You busy? I need to talk with you."

"Sure, come on in. Need something to drink?"

"Water would be fine."

Roger went into the trailer and returned with two bottles of Knobley Mountain Spring Water. "Here you go. A friend of mine in West Virginia owns the company and sends me these." He handed one to Deputy Yates and sat down.

Yates took a sip. "My, that's refreshing. Just what I needed. Sure hits the spot after working out in the sun."

"Yup, I hear my friend up north is doin' well with his business." He paused. "Find anything interesting across the road?"

"Not especially. It was pretty much routine grunt work that needs done to cover all the bases. Got to do a thorough investigation. Don't want to give some defense attorney unnecessary ammo if this thing ever goes to court, do we?"

"That's for sure," Roger said.

Yates looked at him strangely.

"What?" Roger said. "Have I grown a second head or what?"

"You smell like alcohol, and you look like you threw your clothes on in a hurry. What have you been up to?"

"No comment, and I'd like to keep it like that."

"I see. Do yourself a favor and look in the mirror, and stay off the highway. It may not go well for you if you get pulled over."

"Hint taken. I'll stay right here for the rest of the day."

Yates said, "Good. You're thinking better than you look. Are you ready for the storm coming?"

"Storm? What storm?"

"Haven't you been listening to the news or weather? Got an arctic blast coming through. Temperatures are gonna drop to around freezing, maybe below, and 40 to 50 mph winds. Not gonna be fun for a few days while it sticks around."

Roger said, "You serious? I thought it never got cold in Florida?"

"It's pretty rare in central Florida. The panhandle gets it fairly regularly. South Florida almost never, but it does occasionally frost in Miami."

"Guess I better find my space heater. Sounds like I'll need it more than to just take the morning chill off."

"The weatherman says it won't get out of the low forties tomorrow. Think you'll need it most of the day. Won't warm back up for several days. We could get another blast like this before spring arrives, usually around the end of January, but I've seen spells like this all the way into early April."

Roger said, "Thanks for the heads up. I'll batten down the hatches and make sure my critters have cover."

"You should think about getting that tree that shades your trailer cut down or at least trimmed."

"But I like the shade, and I think it's a little late to do anything about it now."

Yates said, "Suit yourself. Be prepared like the Boy Scouts say."

"Gotcha. Any more questions?"

"No. Think I'll be going. Shifts about over and I need to do some prep for what's coming."

"10-4, good buddy. See you on the flip-flop."

Yates smiled and rolled his eyes. "Looks like it's time to go. You take care, Roger, and get prepared. I think it could be one hell of a storm." He started out the door. "Take this serious. It could be a wild night."

"Thanks for the warnin'. You take care and stay safe."

"Will do." Yates walked to his patrol car and soon disappeared down Canaveral Flats Boulevard.

K9 came out from under the trailer.

"Well, girl, you heard it. Winter's comin' in like a lion. Looks like I've got some things to secure so they don't blow away. I'll make sure Donkey's shed's tighty. Don't need no boards or sheet metal breakin' loose and blowin' around."

She barked.

"Yeah, I'll see you and the cat are taken care of, too, though that old cat seems to take care of herself."

She barked again.

"Okay, okay. I'll get to it." He shook his head. "Just like a female to boss me around."

She barked again.

He smiled, "Yes, ma'am," and got to work. The shed did need a few nails for some wall boards and roof sheet metal. He put several concrete blocks on the tarp that covered some plywood and he lowered the shutter that also served to shade the windows in the front of the trailer. The arms holding it up were rusted tight, but a little WD 40 and some of Roger's elbow grease got it loose, down, and secured for the coming storm.

Roger heated a TV dinner for supper, beans and wieners. It was surprisingly tasty. Night came early in the winter, and Roger went to bed early. It had been a busy day. Oh, how he hoped for a quiet night, and the weatherman being wrong. After Yates's warning, he was concerned.

Chapter 12

Roger woke at the crack of dawn, but this morning had no bright awakening, only a dull, threatening gray. He wiped the sleepers from his eyes, stretched, and dressed. He walked out to the porch and saw the ground was wet. The air was still, but had a dangerous, ominous feel to it. K9 came out from under the trailer. "Well, girl, looks like the storm went around us."

Her ears were up. She looked to the west and barked. Roger turned to see what she found interesting and gasped. An ominous shelf cloud stretched across the western sky and it was barreling down on Roger and Canaveral Flats. He swore under his breath. "Dog, that's not lookin' good. Glad I battened down the hatches. You better get in the house with me." Donkey was standing near the shed watching the cloud. K9 barked. "He'll be alright. Donkey's smart enough to get in the shed when the storm hits. Guess the cat's found her a hidey-hole somewhere. She'll be okay. Now, come on inside with me."

She did as told. Roger turned on the radio to an Orlando station, and all he heard was bad news. Report after report told of wind damages-trees blown over, wires down in the streets, and damaged roofs from Tampa on the west coast to Orlando. He looked at the blackening sky that kept getting closer. "Dog, I think we're in for a humdinger of a storm. Out West, they call this a derecho. They're bad news. Better hunker down. This ain't gonna be fun."

He sat on the bench seat in the combined living room-dining room-kitchen, and K9 came to him whimpering. Roger stroked her head and spoke some reassuring words to calm her, but he felt a bit of fear in his heart. He felt the trailer sway in a hard gust. "Easy girl, easy. This won't last forever. Just got to ride it out. Easy does it."

She whined. "Yeah, I'm a little scared, too."

Winds buffeted the ancient trailer as lightning crashed down all around them. Buckets of water pelted the metal walls and roof. A little water dripped from a cloudy skylight.

BOOM!!! K9 yelped, and Roger threw up his hand. Crunch!!! Crash!!! The trailer shook as the roof in the back part of the structure collapsed. A huge tree limb punctured the metal roof. It dangled yellow fiberglass insulation. A curse slipped from Roger's lips. "Hold on, dog. Ain't nothin' we can do now but hold on." He pulled her up to him. Her heart felt like it would beat right out of her chest. "Hang on."

The storm continued to pummel the ancient structure. Water poured through the hole in the roof, and then in an instant, it was calm. Roger looked outside and wondered if there was more coming. He sat speaking calming words to the dog, but he knew he was trying also to calm himself. After about five minutes, he thought it was safe to venture out. As fast as it had come, the storm departed. The porch was intact, but the big oak tree that had shaded the place was now broken in half, and one half was on top of the damaged trailer. The shed roof was missing a piece of sheet metal. Another tree lay on its side, uprooted.

"Well, dog, we made it through the storm, but I think my trailer's toast. I need to get a better look, but it's not lookin' good."

She barked, and Roger walked over the soggy ground around the trailer, assessing the damages. *No, didn't look good at all.* He went inside. A large part of the roof had collapsed and rain water had drenched everything. He sat back down on the bench seat, feeling a little in shock. K9 put her head on his leg. "Yeah, girl. It's bad. I'm not sure what I'm gonna do."

He sat and stroked the dog's head for some time.

"Grrr."

"Someone comin', K9?"

He looked down the driveway. Bill Kenney. No wonder she was growling.

"Looks like your favorite person is here. Behave yourself. We need all the help we can get, even Bill Kenney."

She gave a little ruff, and Roger exited the trailer.

Bill got out of his truck. "You and K9, okay? Your trailer looks bad. That was some storm."

Roger bit his tongue, not saying what was on his mind. *No kidding, Sherlock.* "We're okay, but I think the trailer's ruined."

Bill nodded. "I think you're right. That's my first impression. I got some big tarps. in the back of my truck. Think you and a bunch of people in Canaveral Flats are gonna need them. I'll get one, and we can put a temporary cover over the damages. Try to weatherproof it as much as possible."

Roger said, "That sounds great."

They got the tarp out and, with two ropes thrown over the downed branches, were able to work the tarp over the damaged area. With ropes and Bungee cords, they secured it.

Bill asked, "You sure you're okay? I have to check on several other reports of damages. Haven't got any reports of injuries or trapped people, just trees downed, and roofs damaged. If you're okay, I need to go."

Roger grimaced. "Yeah, I'm okay. K9, too. Go. See who else needs you." He motioned with his hand for Bill to go.

"Okay, call me if you need to. Bye."

"Bye."

Roger sat down and watched Bill drive off. He sighed. "Now what are we gonna do, K9? I'm at a loss for words."

She barked and wagged her tail.

He smiled. "Always the optimist you are, K9, but I don't know what I'm gonna do."

She laid her head on his leg.

"Good girl. Yeah, we'll figure something out."

Chapter 13

"Roger." A moment passed. "Roger."

He opened one bloodshot eye. "Huh? Dog, have you learned to speak?"

"No."

Roger turned to the voice. "Oh, Pastor Nassey. Thought for a moment I might be losin' my mind or hallucinatin'."

Pastor Nassey shook his head. "Looks like you've been drinking. Did it solve your problems?"

"No, just made them go away for a little while. Are my problems still here?"

"In more ways than one. Looks like the storm put a hurting on this place. Mind if I take a look inside?"

"Go ahead. It's a real mess. Chaos reigns."

Pastor opened the door to the trailer and went inside. A minute or so later, he returned to the screened porch and took a chair across from Roger, but said nothing for a long while.

"Well?"

"Well, what?"

"Aren't you gonna say something?" Roger looked at the Pastor, but saw only sorrow and brotherly love in his eyes.

"I feel like Job's friends, only I'm not going to blame you for your problems, except maybe the drinking. Looks like you could use some help."

Roger said, "Yeah, I was beginnin' to wonder if I was beyond hope, or maybe I was jinxed."

"What happened?"

"The storm blew over the tree, and it crashed down on the trailer while me and K9 were in it. Bill Kenney had a tarp, and we covered the damaged area with it. I slept out here on the porch in my La-Z-Boy chair, as I have many times before."

Pastor said, "And tried to drown your problems?"

"Yeah."

"You gonna stay here or not? Place is pretty damaged, probably beyond repair. Got any insurance?"

"On this old firetrap? No, just liability on the property in case someone gets hurt. Insurance on the old tin can would probably cost more than it's worth if I could get it at all." Roger paused to gather his thoughts. "Not sure, but I think I may stay. Bedroom's ruined, but the bathroom still works and the electric does, too."

"Place doesn't look safe."

"It's not. Got any suggestions?"

Pastor thought for a moment. "You may want to talk to a friend of mine, Moe Canard. He owns Moe's Mobile Homes. It's down on US 1 north of Cocoa. He could get you a replacement pretty quick. Tell him I recommended you and I know he'll give you a good deal, but do me one thing."

"What's that?"

"Sober up before you go anywhere." He stopped. "And take a shower. You're a little on the ripe side in more ways than one. How long are you going to keep hitting the bottle every time you have a problem?"

Roger lowered his head and said nothing.

"Chaos, Roger, chaos, you said it earlier. Sometimes this world makes no sense. Your car won't start. You forget an appointment. Your friend has cancer-"

"Or a tree falls on your house, your wife and kid die in a car wreck, or someone tries to kill you on a case you're workin' on."

Pastor said, "All those and more. All the chaos in this world can make us anxious and fearful. It can suck the joy and life out of living for all of us."

"You ever fearful?"

"Yeah, often."

"You don't seem to me to be a fearful person."

"I can let the world press down on my shoulders, or I can choose to live by faith. I believe God's Word, the Bible, is the answer to all of mankind's problems if we would just apply it. We were all created in His image, male and female. Have you ever thought how great a blessing that is?"

Roger smiled. "I still got a tree on my trailer. What do I do?"

"I think you know the answer to that. Put the bottle down. Quit wallowing in your troubles. Do something. Find a solution to your problems, big and small. This world isn't going to change. It will still be a mess tomorrow, just like it is today. Accept that and deal with it. There are a lot of things in this world you can't depend on, but I've found you can always depend on Jesus."

"You know, Pastor, you've been comin' off pretty strong on that God stuff lately."

"Guess I have, but you're a friend, and I want the best for you. We've known each other for some time, and I'm giving you the best advice I know. What kind of a friend would I be if I didn't, and I withheld the best thing I knew from you?"

Roger nodded. "Good point."

They sat in silence for a few moments.

Pastor asked, "So, what are you going to do?"

"Take a nap."

"Take a nap?"

"Yeah, my sleepin' off the night before was interrupted. When I wake up, sober I hope, I grab a bite to eat somewhere, and then I think I'll go down to Moe's and seek new housing. He was recommended by a good friend of mine, and I've found it best to consider, and then follow his wise council."

Pastor rolled his eyes. "Flattery will get you nowhere, Roger, but it does feel good."

"You never did say why you were here."

"I was checking on members of my church to see how they did because of the storm. And other people in Canaveral Flats. Looks like your place got hit the worst."

"Any wonder I have a Job complex?"

Pastor laughed. "But you have better friends."

"Very true."

"Mrs. Tallman lost her carport. As rusty as it was, it's a wonder it stood as long as it did."

Roger asked, "How's she doin'?"

Pastor shook his head. "Not well. Still going downhill. I don't know how she's holding on, but she is. I told her she could let go anytime. She knows the Lord. I know she's suffering so, but she just says, 'Not yet. Not yet.' She never explains why."

"It's hard to figure out."

"It is. I better get going. Roger needs more nappy time."

"Beauty rest, Pastor, beauty rest."

Pastor said, "You'd have to sleep like Rip Van Winkle for even a slight improvement."

"True. Thanks for stoppin' and checkin' on me."

"That's what friends are for." He got up and walked to his car. "See you later, Roger."

"You're always welcome here, Pastor. Bye."

The pastor drove off and Roger was soon asleep dreaming dreams he would not remember with a tortoise-shell cat curled up on his lap. She purred as she slept. Both would need their rest for what was coming soon.

Chapter 14

Roger woke up about 11 o'clock feeling much better, and hungry, very hungry. Also sober enough to drive. He freshened himself up in his intact bathroom in the old trailer, but he had to walk on his knees to get there through the heavily damaged bedroom area.

He got over to Kelsey's Restaurant about 11:30. There weren't too many people seated yet. Several county deputies eyed him, but he paid them no mind. Cops seem to do threat assessments on everyone, and Roger knew he was no exception.

"Roger, over here," a female voice called.

He smiled and walked over to a nearby booth. "Eva, what brings you here?"

"You silly goose, what do you think? Great food and reasonable prices, the same thing that draws so many underpaid law enforcement officers here."

The cops unfolded their arms and smiled, as did Roger.

He sat down. "It's good to see you, Eva. Mind if I sit with you?"

"Go ahead, but I won't be here long. I'm waiting on my order. Should be here soon, but you're welcome to stay."

"I'll do that..."

"Eva, your order is ready," the cashier called.

"I'll be right there," she said. "Roger, I've been wanting to see you. I need to talk to you."

"Sure, I'll be free later this afternoon. I'm in the market for a new trailer. Gonna go look for one after I have my lunch."

"New trailer? Why? What happened?"

"Had a tree fall on my old one in the storm that roared through. The ceiling in the bedroom is now about four and a half feet high and has bark and leaves. I thought about fixing it, but with its age, I decided to replace it with something newer with an intact roof."

She said, "Sorry to hear of your misfortune. Looks like you're okay. Did your animals get hurt?"

"They all came through unharmed."

"That's good to know. Roger, I really must go. The cashier's getting anxious. Is about four o'clock good with you?"

"Sounds fine. I'll see you then."

She smiled. "See you around four." She got up, paid for her order, smiled at Roger, and left.

Wonder what she needs to see me about? Guess I'll find out later today.

Roger had a sandwich and a small salad, but no alcohol. No hair of the dog today. The cops left shortly before he did. Traffic on US 1 was moderate as he made his way down to Moe's just north of the town of Cocoa. Moe had a nice selection of trailers.

Roger heard someone call to him as he inspected the trailers. "Can I help you?"

"Well, yeah. I need one of these as soon as possible. Just not sure which one."

The man walked up and held his hand out. "Joe Morris at your service. What were you looking for today?"

"I need something I can get into in a hurry. That bad storm that went through dropped a tree on my old trailer, and I have to replace it. I was told by a friend I should ask for Moe. He'd treat me right and give me a good deal."

The young man smiled. "Moe's my dad. He's out on an errand. He won't be back today, but I can help you. Give me an idea what you're looking for."

Roger said, "I've got an old travel trailer now, about a 30-footer. I'm not sure exactly what I want, but something bigger. Probably a small trailer, two bedrooms and a real hallway, not a walk-through."

"Well, we've got several like that or similar. Would you like me to show them to you, or you could walk around until you saw something interesting and inspect at your own pace? All the trailers are open, unlocked. What would you like?"

"I think I'll do the latter."

Joe said, "Suit yourself. If you need help, I'll be between here and the office. If you see another person walking around like he owns the place about my age, that would be my brother, Beau."

Roger said, "Moe, Joe, and Beau. You all rhyme."

Joe laughed, "Yeah, we do even without our sister, Ro, as in Rowena. She's our bookkeeper. You may see her in the office."

"What's your mother's name, Flo?"

Joe smiled, "No, it's Frances. Mom goes by Fanny. And no, she doesn't work here. She's busy at home taking care of her elderly mother, my grandmother, Chloe, but yes, she goes by Chlo."

"I knew there had to be another rhymer around here. Tell you what, I'll get to lookin' for something I like, I'll find you, and then we can talk turkey. Sound good?"

"Sounds good. Take your time. We're open till five. And if you don't find something that tickles your fancy, we can order you something, but that could take a while to get in."

"I need something today. It won't take that long for me to decide."

The two men parted, and Roger worked his way among the large selection. Like Goldilocks, he checked three out, too big, too small, just the right size. The last he guessed was about 40 to 45 feet, with two bedrooms, a bath, a small utility area, a hallway, and a combination living room-kitchen-dining room. There were three similar to choose from. The two in the front were new and smelled so. The floor layout on one seemed odd, but the other was fine, but Roger didn't like the chemical smell inside. The last was used and had a little wear, but didn't have any smells, good or bad.

Roger found Joe, and they went over the pluses and minuses of that trailer. Yes, it was used, but not abused. Joe assured him everything worked and there were no leaks in the plumbing or the roof. Roger explained how he needed his old damaged trailer out of the way and the new one put in the same place, and all in one day ASAP. Joe said they could do that, possibly do it not tomorrow, but the next day. They agreed on a price and a time. Roger wrote a check. Told Joe to check with the bank to make sure it was good. Any problems, contact him immediately. They shook hands, and Roger headed for home. Eva would be there soon. *Wonder what she wanted?*

Chapter 15

"Ruff."

"Yeah, I see the car. I'm expectin' someone, a friend. You be good."

She wagged her tail. The car stopped, and Eva got out. It didn't take her long to get through the dummy locked gate and to Roger's damaged trailer.

"Hello, Roger," she said as she neared the trailer. "Is it as bad as it looks?"

"Worse. I just bought a replacement, one a little bigger and newer. Should be here soon. Come on in and have a seat. Can I get you anything?"

"Water would be fine." She opened the screen door of the porch, and K9 greeted her. "Oh, my. You're so happy. Good girl. Have you been keeping Roger out of trouble?"

"That she has. You and K9 have a happy time meeting and greeting, and I'll get you that water."

"Sure thing."

Roger slid by Eva and K9, went in the trailer, and returned with two bottles of water. "Here you go."

"Thank you." She took a seat in a folding aluminum chair with nylon straps and took a sip. "Refreshing."

"Best I know of. A friend in West Virginia owns this company and sends me cases at a time."

She said, "It's good to have friends. What would we do without them? Are you doing alright? Do you need anything?"

"I'm managin' right now. I was feelin' a little down earlier this morning, and Pastor Nassey came around and gave me a pep talk. I needed it."

"We all need it sometimes. Without hope, we die." She shifted in her seat. "You know how I told you about being a prisoner in a Nazi concentration camp?"

"Yes, I remember. We talked a lot about your experiences there. A hellish time."

She nodded, "It was Sheol. May it never happen again, but it could. The heart of man is cold, but even in times of unimaginable troubles, some have hope. Can I tell you a story, an intense story that's still being written?"

"Sure. I could use a story of hope right now."

She cleared her throat. "Do you remember the part of me telling you about being the camp commander's slave, her Pet she called me, and being able to walk about the camp fairly freely? It was one of the few privileges I had for being her slave. No one bothered me because they feared the commander's wrath, as I did, too."

"Yes, I remember our talk."

"My mind kept taking me back to the political prisoner's barracks, and to the Dutch women I saw praying. Corrie Ten Boom had to be one of them. I told you about finding her book, *The Hiding Place,* about her experiences at Ravenbrück camp. That book spoke to me, and I couldn't get it out of my mind. How could she and others have hope with all the death and human depravity going on around them? You could die at any moment. Guards beat people to death and threw them in the gas chambers because they felt like it. I only survived because I would do whatever the commandant wanted without complaint. She protected me from the others there, but the things I had to do for her and with her were shameful, but I wanted to live. I was so afraid of dying. Corrie and her friends didn't want to die either, but they didn't fear death like I did."

Roger nodded.

She had his full attention and continued, "Do you believe in angels?"

"Can't say I ever seen one."

"Not sure I have either, but those women in there in the Dutch barrack sure seemed to have a divine comforter with them. They never seemed abandoned or alone."

She shifted in the chair. "Roger, you know me, the old atheist. How could there be a god when there's so much misery and hurting in this world, yet finding her book and remembering what happened at the camp raised questions that chipped away at my doubt. I've talked with Rabbi Katz about it, faith and hope. He gave me some answers, but Pastor Nassey gave me better answers, and you know where he's coming from. I told him I wanted to figure it all out. He laughed and said when I did to tell him, but I wouldn't be able. It's bigger than me or you. God isn't asking us to figure it all out. He's asking us to trust that He already has. Even though my life may have more ups and down, twists and turns than a rollercoaster. Sometimes it's a grand adventure. Other times, it's sheer terror, but some people, like Pastor Nassey, believe God's got it all under control. He's never surprised and is working it all out in His good timing."

Neither said anything for a few moments.

Roger sighed. "That's some real truth bombs. Did he press you on that Jesus thing?"

"No, he didn't have to. It was written all over the place, and that's the truth."

"The truth be told, the truth is seldom told. We say we're fine, but we're falling apart inside. Everyone's life is perfect but ours."

She said, "Very true. This was the conversation I wanted to say to you face to face, without anyone else around."

Roger smiled, "We have K9 listening, but she's good at keepin' a confidence."

"I wanted someone I knew to tell this to. It's hard to be honest with some people, but you, I trust."

"So, what are you gonna do now?"

"I don't know. Think some more and see where it takes me. Sooner or later, probably sooner, I'll come to the point where I'll know I've thought enough, and it's time to make a decision."

Roger sighed. "Yeah. That's heavy duty."

"Yeah, you're telling me." She stopped. "Roger, I need to go."

"I understand. Thanks for stopping in. Do it again when you need a confidant."

She got up. "I will. Bye."

"Bye." Roger watches as she walked to her car and drove off.

Life sure does feel like you're riding the biggest and baddest rollercoaster there is.

"Hello, white man."

Roger jumped. "Shaman! How long have you been here?"

"Danger, white man, danger." The Shaman turned and disappeared into the brush.

Roger swore under his breath. *Now what?*

Chapter 16

"Huh?" Roger said. "Leave me alone. I'm tryin' to sleep. Go away," but K9 continued to pull on his pants leg. "Go away, I said." She kept on pulling and made a snarling and guttural sound with the blue jean fabric she clutched in her teeth.

"K9, go way. It's o dark thirty. Please leave me alone," but she continued the strange behavior. "Dammit, K9." He opened his eyes. It was not dark, but fiery. He looked around. His trailer was on fire. His trailer was on fire? His trailer was on fire! He swore as he jumped up. "K9, get outta here!"

Roger slipped his shoes on and did a quick survey of the situation. Fire ate through the blue tarp covering the roof. The heat on his face told him to grab what he could and get out now. He found the cell phone on the table next to him and ran out the porch door. The heat was following him and getting hotter. He started his truck and drove it away, leaving it near Donkey's shed. Donkey intently watched the fire burn.

Roger got out of his truck and called 911 on his cell phone. He told them of his emergency and the location. Yes, everyone got out. Yes, he'd open the gate when the firemen arrived, but he didn't think they needed to hurry. His trailer was totally consumed by fire and going up fast. After hanging up, he found a stump, sat down, and sighed. K9 came to him and whined.

"Yeah, K9, it's gone Won't be nothing left but a pile of twisted metal." She laid her head on his leg and sighed. "It's okay, girl. We got out. I got a replacement comin', but we may need a place to stay for several days."

"Ruff."

"Looks like I'll need everything to start over, not that I had much of anythin' worth cryin' over. Guess I'll need some clothes, toiletries, and some more food. New trailer has a real stove and even a small washer and dryer. It'll be high cotton."

"Ruff."

"Yeah, I won't forget the dog food." He paused and wiped a tear from his eye. "Still gonna miss the old place. Lotta good memories."

"Ruff."

"Yeah, girl. I agree. We need some marshmallows. Not much we can do, but watch it burn."

They watched as the flames leaped higher.

K9 stood up. "Ruff."

He heard the distant sound of a fire truck approaching. When he saw the flashing lights, he walked to the gate and let them in. A young man drove the truck down to the fire. Several other young people got out and rapidly began unrolling hoses. A man about Roger's age got out of the truck and walked back to meet him.

"You the homeowner?"

"Yeah, I own what's left of the old trailer."

"Did everyone get out?"

"There's just me and my critters and we're all accounted for."

"That's good." He held out his hand, which Roger shook. "I'm Dan Walsh, captain of this bunch from Four Communities Volunteer Fire Department. You are..."

"Roger Pyles. If you see a dog, that's K9. She's good natured. Seems to like everyone, with the exception of, maybe, Bill Kenney."

Dan laughed. "Yeah, old Bill has rubbed a few people the wrong way." He turned and shouted, "Hey, Bobby. Hose down those hot spots. Tell the others."

"Sure thing, chief."

They watched as the crew began to hose down the fire.

Roger said, "Don't seem much reason to waste water fightin' it now."

Dan nodded. "There's not. Got a bunch of new recruits and they're all eager to do something. This will be good training for them. They'll need it when we run up against a difficult fire. Got to break 'em in on something easy so they get a feel for it. Sorry it had to be you. You do know you could contact the Red Cross for help with a temporary place to stay and some provisions?"

"I hadn't thought that far ahead. Still feel a little in shock from seein' it burn. Just happy no one was hurt."

They watched as the newbie volunteers learned to operate the equipment. For the most part, they did a good job, but a hose got away from a young woman, and water flew everywhere. Dan ran and shut the line off and then gave the frightened and embarrassed volunteer some pointers. She went back to hosing down the fire, and he walked back to Roger and smiled.

Dan said, "I figured that might happen. The girls want to do what the boys are doing. They have heart but lack the strength of the boys. Sometimes we can show them ways to compensate for that, but not always. Still, I'm glad to have them along. Volunteers are getting harder and harder to find."

Roger nodded. They watched as the firemen worked and gained experience. After an hour or so, the fire died down, and they mopped up what was left. When satisfied, it was safe and they could do no more; the volunteers left in their big red truck.

"Well, K9, what's we gonna do?"

She barked.

"I should have known. We improvise just like Doctor Who does."

They walked around the trailer and saw a few glowing ashes and then went to Roger's truck. "Hop in, girl. I get the cramped seat, and you get the floor. Maybe we can get a few hours of shuteye."

She circled once, laid down, and was soon asleep, as was Roger. They'd need their energy for the day ahead.

Chapter 17

"Ruff."

Roger stretched and yawned. Sunlight flooded his bleary eyes. *What time is it?* He looked at his watch, 9 o'clock. How could he have slept this long with it being so bright? But he had. K9 danced in the truck. "Okay, girl, I get the picture. Full bladder. You have to pee."

He opened the door, and K9 rushed out. She squatted down and relieved herself. Roger sat up and ran his fingers through his hair. He yawned again, put his shoes on, got out of the truck, and watered the grass. "Ah, so much better, K9. Thought my eyeballs were floatin'."

He looked at the old trailer. A little smoke drifted skyward from what used to be his bedroom. K9 walked up beside him and whimpered. "Yeah, girl, it really happened. It wasn't a bad dream. Looks like we're homeless."

He walked around the debris, but there wasn't much left. Even his La-Z-Boy chair on the porch was little more than charred wood and springs. After checking the aluminum porch door handle for hotness and finding it was only warm, he opened it and went in. K9's food in the metal garbage can used to store it seemed okay, a little smoky, but he nearly burned his hand on the hot handle. K9 eagerly ate the food he put in her dish.

The trailer seemed a total loss. The landline phone on the porch was nothing but melted plastic. *Glad I have my cell phone.* "K9, you stay here and guard what's left of the place. I'm gonna go get some breakfast and try to figure out an immediate plan of action. Looks like my plans from yesterday have changed, and I got a lot more to do."

K9 kept eating. She wagged her tail, but never looked up.

"Yeah, I'm hungry, too, famished."

He walked to his truck and got in. After going ten feet, it shut off and a cloud of dark, nasty smelling smoke poured from under the hood. "Oh, no." He sat there as the smoke cleared, and tried to start it again. Nothing, absolutely nothing. He popped the hood and looked around, but saw nothing out of the ordinary. He tried to start it again, but it refused to even turn over. No clicking, no nothing. It sat there like a two-ton paperweight.

Roger sighed and gave the dash a halfhearted whack with his fist. *What else can go wrong?* He reached for his cell phone and opened it. *One percent charge!* Quickly, he dialed the number for his favorite local shade tree mechanic. He heard the phone ring twice, and then it went dead. The screen was black. He shook his head. *I'm beginnin' to know how Job felt. Please, Lord, no more misfortunes today.*

He sighed. *I feel like I've got a black cloud followin' me around.* He sighed again, but deeper. *Now what?*

"Grrr."

"What's up, girl?"

"Grrr."

A truck was approaching on Canaveral Flats Boulevard. As it got closer, Roger knew why K9 was growling: Bill Kenney.

Lord, did you just bless me with a friend comin' to comfort me? Please, none like Job's friends.

"Grrr."

"You be good. Right now, I could use any help I can get. No bitin'."

Bill parked his truck on the road's shoulder and walked to meet Roger.

"When did this happen?" Bill asked.

"Last night. I didn't get a whole lot of sleep after the firemen left. Me and K9 slept in my truck. I was just leavin', but my truck broke down, my cell phone's dead, and you show up. Where were you last night? Thought you'd show up and check out what was goin' on."

"I'm just getting back from Tampa. I've been over on the west coast for several days getting training on how to tell when someone is lying. The class was taught by an ex-CIA guy. It was well worthwhile." He stopped. "Uh, you're in quite a pickle. What's you gonna do?"

"Can you help?"

"Sure, what are friends for? What do you need first?"

Roger said, "Breakfast would be nice. I salvaged some food for K9, but my kitchen and pantry are gone."

"I'll take you to my place. Hope you don't mind a frozen breakfast."

"Not at all. I could eat a horse, raw if necessary."

Bill laughed. "No horse meat, but I do have a bacon, eggs, and potatoes bowl."

"Super, what are we waitin' for?"

Bill took Roger to his house and microwaved two breakfast bowls, one for Roger and one for himself. The ride from Tampa had made him hungry. A cup of hot coffee finished out the meal. Afterward, they went to the couch.

Bill said, "How about telling me what's happened with you since I've been away?"

Roger said, "Well, it's been a lot of bad news for me. First the big windstorm blew the tree down on my house. I knew it was ruined, so I went to Moe's Trailers in Cocoa and bought another one. It'll be a couple of days before they can get it here and set it up. My porch was pretty much still intact, so I slept on it last night until K9 woke me up because the old place was on fire."

"Good old K9."

"The firemen came and did what they could, not much. It was already about gone when they got there. They left about four A.M., so me and K9 slept in my truck until about nine when the call of nature awakened both of us."

Bill said, "I'm learning more about that early morning call as I get older."

"I checked out the damages in the daylight. K9's dog food was the only thing I saw salvageable. I told you about the truck takin' a dump on my way to breakfast, tryin' to call Scott, but the cell phone died, and then you showed up."

"So here we are. What's you gonna do now?"

"Try to contact some people and see if I can get some stuff done. Looks like I'm homeless and without transportation and hopin' nothing else goes wrong." Roger stopped. "Aren't you goin' to work today?"

"I took the morning off. Don't have to start till noon. You can stay here. Use my phone, okay. You may want to talk to Suzie.

She's working the afternoon shift. She likes to sleep late, but should be up about the time I leave."

"Thanks, Bill. I appreciate it. I'm kinda between a rock and a hard spot."

"Go ahead and make your calls. I need to run to the grocery store. Need anything?"

Roger said, "I need everything, but one thing at a time. Let me check on gettin' transportation first."

"Sure thing. Make yourself at home while I'm gone."

"Will do. Thanks."

Bill left, and Roger made phone calls. Scott, the mechanic, agreed to check out Roger's dead truck. Moe was busy delivering and setting up a mobile home, but Roger got to talk to Joe. He had bad news for Roger. The trailer he wanted had been damaged, both inside and out. A drunk ran off the highway the night after the storm and driven right through it and half way through another. The trailer was a total loss, but he could get him another slightly bigger one for $200 more right now. Roger remembered the other trailer and said yes. That would work.

Roger felt like his luck might be improving. He could use some good news for a change. What more could go wrong? He didn't want to know.

Chapter 18

Oh, my head hurts. And the rest of me don't feel so good either.

Roger opened his bleary eyes and looked around.

This place looks familiar, but it ain't home. Where am I?

It had been a long time since he felt this bad and wasn't drunk. Slowly, it came to him. He was at Bill's place and that funny smell was him.

Lord have mercy. What's goin' on?

He wasn't sure of a lot of things, but one thing he did know for sure was his bladder was full and about to overflow. As he dropped his feet to the floor, his head began to spin. He laid his back against the couch and braced himself with his arms. Gradually, the spinning stopped. He sat for a moment as his thoughts cleared.

What am I doin' here?

Then he remembered the fire.

What day is it? He looked at Bill's wall calendar with days past crossed off. *What? Can't be. The fire happened four days ago. Where had the time gone? Was someone playin' a trick on him?*

If one thing was certain, his bladder was screaming for relief. Gingerly, he got up and stumbled his way to the bathroom. After taking care of business, he found his way back to the living room. The clock said twelve. It was light outside, so it had to be noon.

What's goin' on?

He heard someone moving in the efficiency, a barrel lock on the door being unbolted. It opened, and Suzie appeared.

She said, "Well, Rip Van Winkle. We were wondering when you would wake up? How do you feel?"

"Like I got hit by a truck. What's been goin' on?'

She rolled her eye. "Roger Pyles, you are about the most stubborn man I've ever known."

"I get it from Donkey."

"I think it's the other way around. Just saying. How do you feel? You gave us a scare."

Roger said, "What did I do? Run naked down Canaveral Flats Boulevard howling at the moon?"

"Yes."

"Yes? No way, though I seem at a loss in fillin' in the recent past." He paused. "I really didn't run naked down the road, did I? I did some streakin' while I was in college, but there was a bunch of us at that time." He stopped again. "Did I really run naked?"

"No, you've hardly moved from that couch for the last four days. About the only thing you've done is sleep, moan occasionally, drink a little water and Gatorade, and find the bathroom. Don't you remember?"

He thought about her question. "No."

"I'm not surprised. You were out of it."

Roger said nothing. "Four days? Guess that's why I smell so bad."

"I've smelled you like this before when we were young, cousin, and I was living at your house."

Roger said, "Back when your parents were havin' problems."

"Yeah, you'd run some water in the tub, splash your hand through it, wait a while, and tell your mom you were done."

"Yeah, I remember. She finally got wise to me. Told me she could grow taters in my ears. She picked me up, took me to the bathroom, striped me down, and scrubbed me like I'd never been scrubbed before. Think I lost a layer of skin."

"I remember. She never shut the door. I watched and laughed, and your father was there to back up your mom."

"It was kind of humiliating. I learned to lie better to my mom, but she still had a way of figurin' out when I was."

Suzie smiled. "Moms are good at knowing when their kids are lying. And Roger, you really need a bath. You'd repulse a skunk."

"That bad?"

"Maybe worse."

"You gonna scrub me if I say no?"

She said, "I'd do it with a wire brush. Bill would help along with several other men we'd round up."

"No need for that. I'll go voluntarily. I can hardly stand myself, but I see a problem."

"What?"

Roger said, "I got no clean clothes, and everything at my place burned up in the fire."

"You shower up, and I'll find something for you to cover up with while I wash your clothes."

"Okay, thanks."

Roger got up slowly and hobbled to the bathroom. He shut the door, striped, cracked the door open, and dropped all his dirty clothes in the hallway. "Here you go, Suz."

She picked up his soiled clothing and said, "Nice hiney, just like I remember, only bigger."

"You can't see me. I'm behind the door."

"You forgot the full-length mirror behind you."

"Oh."

Roger shut the door and turned on the shower. When the water got warm, he climbed in and washed the grunge down the drain. He found a clean towel and dried off, then wrapped another one around his waist and walked out. Suzie met him.

"Here." She handed him a pair of shorts and a T-shirt. "These should be big enough for you. Try them on."

"No underwear?"

"Didn't think you wanted any Bill'd worn."

Roger said, "Good point."

Roger changed in the bathroom. When he came out, he smelled something pleasant. The odor came from the kitchen. *Breakfast!* "That smells good. I'm hungry."

Suzie said, "Good. You haven't eaten since you got here."

"What's that I smell, coffee?"

"It is. Can't say I drink it, so I hope it's passable."

Roger said, "Right now, used motor oil would be passable." He poured a cup and took a sip. "Not bad, Suz, not bad."

Suzie cooked some bacon, put it next to the scrambled eggs and a bagel. "Here you go."

"Thanks."

They ate hungrily in silence.

Roger burped. "My compliments to the chef. That was good."

"Don't expect it every day. Bill and me are getting tired of caring for you."

"So, it really was four days I've been here."

"Four long days caring for sick, pain in the butt, Roger."

"I'm not that bad."

"Worse. Be glad you have friends and family you can depend on."

Roger said, "Thanks. Fill me in about what I missed."

"We tried to get you to go to a doctor, but you refused. You're more stubborn than Donkey, but you owe your recovery to him."

"Huh? What?"

Suzie said, "Bill saw a strange truck at your property and investigated. Turns out it was Doctor Solomon, the vet. He was there to check out your donkey."

"I forgot about that, but why do I owe my recovery to Donkey?"

"Doc wanted to know where you were. Bill told him sick on his couch. He asked what were your symptoms. Bill told him, and he gave Bill some pills, office samples he used to treat animals."

Roger said, "I took donkey pills?"

"Yeah, but doc adjusted them for your weight. Hey, this nurse and the vet know most meds that work on animals will also work on people. What other choice did we have? You wouldn't go to a doctor. What worked for one ass should work on another."

Roger grimaced, "Donkey pills. Has anyone been checkin' on my critters while I was down for the count?"

"Lester's been feeding them. He's making sure your new trailer is set up properly. They got it all done but the skirting. Hope you wanted a new screened-in porch."

Roger said, "Good ole Lester," and he smiled.

"Your truck's outside. Scott looked it over. You had a short in one of your battery cables. He fixed it."

"Good ole Scott."

"Don't forget me and Bill. We housed you and nursed you back to health in spite of yourself."

"Good old Suzie, and it pains me to say this, but good old Bill."

"Yup, you can depend on your friends."

Roger was silent for a moment. "Thanks."

"What was that?"

Roger repeated, "Thanks. I'm more blessed than I realize."

"We all are, Roger. Everyone has hard times. You just got to get through them."

"Yeah, you'd know."

She said, "You, too." She sighed.

"I should give you a hug."

"Spare me until you get better."

Roger said, "Okay."

"You feeling well enough to go to your new home?"

"Think I'll catch a few more winks, and then go."

"Sounds good."

Roger cleaned the table and walked to the living room.

Suzie washed their dishes and the ones already in the sink Bill left. She found Roger asleep on the couch snoring. She smiled. *If he's still here when Bill gets home, he's Bill's problem, not mine. Hope they both behave themselves.*

Chapter 19

Roger woke several hours later feeling better. A quick look at the clock told him it was four in the afternoon. He made a quick trip to the bathroom. Done, he washed his hands and looked in the mirror. "Good grief, you look bad, but you looked worse a few hours ago."

He ran his finger through his hair and had some success taming the unruly mass. "There, better."

He made his way to the utility room and heard the dryer going round and round, squeaking each time as it turned. *Needs new slides.* He opened the door and hot air hit his face as the drum slowed and finally stopped. Roger shook his head. *That Bill. Wonder if he ever cleans the lint trap? He could start a fire, and I betcha I'd get blamed. Bet he'd say I was some kinds jinx.*

With his hand, he scooped out the glob of lint and threw it in the trash. The clothes were still damp, but he found that a shirt and one pair of underwear were dry enough to wear. He stripped his clothes off and began to button the shirt.

"Roger, are you going to make it a habit of running around naked here?"

"Suzie! How long have you been there?"

"Long enough. Would you get decent?" She turned and left.

Roger hurriedly put on his underwear. He checked his blue jeans, but they weren't dry. He tossed them back in the dryer and started it. Bill's shorts were even tighter than before now he had on his underwear. He walked to the living room where Suzie stood. She rolled her eyes.

"What?" Roger said. "Now what?"

"I tried not to notice and say anything before, but those short pants are as tight as the ones the Chippendale strippers start out with, only you're going in reverse, naked to tight pants."

"You really know how to make a guy feel good." He paused. "How would you know about the Chippendales?"

She grinned. "I'll never tell. Seriously Roger, I wouldn't go out in public like that. Those shorts are pretty tight and don't leave much to the imagination. There's no question about you being a boy."

"Okay, I get the drift, Suzie. Just the same, I don't think I'm up to servicing every female who'd be unable to resist and threw themselves at me."

She laughed and rolled her eyes. "I think you're feeling better. Your sense of humor is coming back."

He sighed. "Yeah, I'm feelin' a little better. Don't think I'm up to whippin' my weight in wildcats unless they were newborns, though a horny woman could be what the doctor ordered."

Suzie shook her head. "Men. A horny woman would probably kill you right now, in the shape you're in."

"Probably, but at least I'd die happy."

She gave him a dirty look. "I think you're well enough to go."

"I believe so, too, or else I might get thrown out."

Suzie said, "You got that right."

"Thanks for watchin' over me when I was down and doin' my clothes. What can I do to repay you?"

She grinned. "I'll think of something. I'll see you get the rest when they're dry." She put her hands on her hips. "Now, just go before I'm tempted to grab your ear and drag you to the door."

Roger said, "No need for that. I know the story. Fish and guest stink after four days."

She nodded. "It's **three** days. You better get going. Don't forget your cell phone. I recharged it for you."

"Thanks. I appreciate all you guys have done, even though I may not be very good at showin' it."

"Roger, have you ever been told you're a pain in the butt?"

"Often, but they usually use more colorful language."

Suzie said, "Yeah, you're feeling better."

"Better go. Thanks for your help." Roger grabbed his cell phone from a nearby table and headed for the door. "See you later. Bye"

"Take care, cuz. Bye."

Roger walked to his truck and got in. He put the key in the ignition switch, and the old truck engine fired right up. He drove over to his property. Donkey gave him no hassle as he opened and closed the gate and drove to the new trailer that sat where the old one had been. The burned-out remains were nearby. As he got out, K9 came running to him. She gave a happy dance at his feet.

"Good girl. You sure are happy to see me. No wonder dogs are man's best friend. If a man had been gone for four days, his woman would never have let him forgot it." He rubbed her head and back. "I've missed you, too. You seen the cat anywhere?"

She gave a woof sound.

"That's what I thought."

Roger walked around the new trailer inspecting it, with K9 following him. Whoever'd done the setup had done a good job. He climbed the aluminum stairs and tried the doorknob. It was unlocked, and he went on in, as did K9. It was a little bigger than he remembered, but he liked that. He tried the lights, and they came on. Then he turned on the faucet at the sink, and the water flowed.

"Well, K9. Looks like we're in business."

The new trailer was empty except for a couch in the living room/kitchen/great room that showed some wear.

"Let's go, girl. Got to check on the donkey and a few other things outside."

She gave a wolf and followed him outside and to Donkey's lean-to shed. Donkey was there, and K9 kept Roger between her and the donkey, though Donkey made no move toward her. Someone had made sure he was well provided for.

Roger walked across the road and then on his other property. The dirt was leveled out and compacted, even the area in the back where the crime scene tape had been. It was ready for a house.

"To build or not to build. That is the question. And if so, what kind?"

K9 growled.

"What's wrong? You don't like Shakespeare? I didn't slaughter him that bad, did I?"

She growled again, and he saw why she was acting out.

Bill Kenney drove up and stopped. "Good to see you're up and off my couch. How you feeling?"

"Better, but wearing down fast. Feel like I need a nap."

"Got something for you." He handed Roger a large paper bag with a Winn Dixie logo on the side. "Here's your pants. Put them on. Those shorts could get you arrested for indecent exposure."

Roger said, "Yeah, they are kinda tight. Fit you pretty good, but not me. Thanks, and thanks for you guys taking care of me."

"You're welcome. How's the new place?"

"Ready to live in, but empty except for a couch."

Bill said, "Lester found it. Some people were moving and couldn't take it. I helped him get it in. Had a devil of a time getting it in the trailer door."

"I bet you did. Thanks."

"Got to go. I'm on patrol."

Roger said, "Sure thing. Bye and thanks again."

Bill waved and was off. As Roger walked to the new trailer, he realized how tired he was. He stuck his head under the kitchen sink faucet and took a long drink. Tomorrow, he'd need to get some cups and just about everything else. He had nothing, not even toilet paper and soap.

He sat on the couch and sighed. K9 laid down at his feet. "Girl, there's so much to do and whatever this crud I've got is, it isn't done kicking my butt."

She closed her eyes, and Roger did, too. A few minutes later, they were both asleep. His immediate needs would have to wait for later.

Chapter 20

Roger woke the next morning while it was still dark. A quick look at his watch told him he'd been asleep for almost fourteen hours. He couldn't believe how long he'd slept. After yawning and nearly tripping over K9, he found his way to his new bathroom. Feeling a little groggy, he sat on his toilet and urinated. Fortunately, all he passed was gas. It was after that, Roger realized he had no toilet paper. He thought about his situation for a moment. "Better get some of that as soon as the stores open. Don't like the idea of makin' like an Arab in the desert."

He stumbled around in the dark until he found a light switch, but nothing happened. No light. He tried several more with the same results. *Looks like light bulbs were not included in the deal.* After working his way to the couch, he thought about his predicament. *Surely, there had to be some source of light. The kitchen. The kitchen probably had a fluorescent light. There had to be a switch around there somewhere.* After much searching, he found a switch, flipped it, and a light came on. "Thank you, Jesus and Florida Power and Light. Better add some light bulbs and toilet paper to my gotta get list," he said just to hear a human voice.

He explored his new trailer and made plans on where he could store items in closets and cabinets. There was a lot of empty space he could fill throughout the whole dwelling. A quick look at his watch told him McDonald's would open in about an hour. Roger looked at K9. "I got nothing to eat here, girl. Think I'll get dressed and head on over. Be there when the door opens. Egg McMuffin and coffee sounds pretty good right now." K9 barked. "No, girl, you have your dog food. About the only thing we could salvage, but I better get some more. Looked like we were gettin' kinda low."

He sighed. "So much to do and I'm still feelin' pretty rotten." He found the bottle of pills that had been in the paper bag with his pants. *Got to be what they'd been treating me with. No label? No instructions?* He shrugged his shoulders, got a glass of water, and took two.

"K9, I'm headin' out now. You guard the place, but there's nothing here any self-respecting thief would want." K9 followed him out. "I won't be too long. Get my breakfast and come back. Stores won't be open for several more hours."

He walked to his truck and got in. A movement around the blocks supporting the trailer caught his eye. The cat was back, and she doesn't look too worse for wear. *A little skinnier, maybe. Probably been hidin' out after all the excitement.* With stealth, she made her way through the doggy dog in the porch screen door toward K9's bowl. *That Lester thought of everything, even a door for K9.* The cat began to eat from it. Roger started the truck, and she took off like a shot. Roger shook his head. "Sorry, kitty. Guess we're all on edge."

Traffic was light as he drove to the fast-food restaurant. He had to wait several minutes for the door to open. A woman in a car with three kids pulled up. Roger could tell they were living in their car from the appearance. A woman came to the restaurant door and unlocked it. He went in and ordered. He handed the cashier a twenty and said, "There's a woman sittin' in her car outside with her kids. Looks to me like they're callin' it home. Take what's left of that twenty and use it on her order, okay?"

The young man said he understood. Roger's order came quickly. He went outside and sat in his truck. He watched as she went inside with the kids and ordered. When she tried to pay, the cashier refused her money. She seemed confused, but appeared to be thanking the McDonald's employee. They turned to Roger. He smiled, and then the woman ran outside to Roger, who was trying to back out.

"Señor. Gracias. Thank you so much. I only had enough money to feed my babies. Thank you. Thank you."

Roger said, "It's okay, ma'am. I've had a run of bad luck lately myself. I'm glad I could help someone else and try to forget some of my problems."

"Thank you so. God bless you, Señor." Tears flowed down her face.

"You're welcome, ma'am."

She went inside and sat with her children. Her back was toward Roger. He got out of his truck and went back inside to the young man who had served them.

"Young man," he said, "You're gonna help me help that woman and her kids. Give her this when she's leavin." He handed him a twenty. "Do you understand?" The young man said he did. "Good, because if I find out you didn't, I'll find you and kick your sorry thievin' ass across US 1 and all the way to the Indian River. You're sure you understand?" The young man swallowed hard and said he did. "Very good. An ass kickin's not worth twenty dollars. You have a nice day."

Roger got in his truck, grabbed his coffee, and took a sip. *Glad that kid don't know how bad I feel. Not sure I could take him today.* A satisfied grin came to his face, and he saw the pimple faced youth staring at him. Roger smiled menacingly and then drove off into the darkness. He munched on the Egg McMuffin as he drove. The sun peeked above the horizon as he stopped at his new trailer.

Tasty sandwich, but I don't feel so good. Gotta be some kind of virus. I'm goin' back to bed. Hope I feel better later.

Chapter 21

"Hey, Roger. Open the door, or do we have to break it down?"

Roger rolled over on his couch. *Got to be a bad dream.* Why would anyone want to break his door down? He hadn't done anything wrong. *Maybe it was bad guys out there after him. Why hadn't K9 barked? Was she dead?* He woke from his dream world with a start. He'd done everything right. Had to be some of the bad guys he'd tracked down. *I need a gun,* but the one he had burned up in the fire.

He wasn't going down without a fight. *How many were there?* He thought he remembered hearing vehicles before, but it was just part of the dream, right? No, there were people outside, and they wanted him.

Was there something he could use as a club? He looked around. Nothing. *Guess I do this hand to hand.* Bleary-eyed, he crawled from the couch, stole a glance out the front window, and saw about ten people, mainly seniors, and about half were women. *What?*

"Roger, are you okay, or do we have to break in? I'm tired of hollering. Open up. Are you sick or dead or deaf or all the above?"

Roger's sleepy brain began to function, and he recognized the voice, Pastor Nassey. Relieved, he went to the door and opened it. "Hello."

Ten sets of eyes looked at him. Some had a look of concern on their faces. Some were smiling, but none looked threatening. No one here seemed to want to harm him.

Roger ran his hand through his hair, attempting to comb the unruly mass. "Pastor Nassey, how long have you been here?"

He answered, "About five minutes. We were beginning to worry about your well-being. Are you okay?"

"About half asleep and recoverin' from a very rotten cold. Other than that, I'm okay, on the mend. What brings all you good people here today?"

"We want to bless you. These people are deacons, elders, and their wives from my church. I mentioned you and your string of bad luck to them at our meeting yesterday. They remembered you'd stop in for services on occasion, and they wanted to bless you. Help out someone in need. Are you up for a blessing?"

Roger said nothing for a moment. He felt confused. "A blessing? You guys want to bless me? Why? How?"

Pastor Nassey said, "I stopped out here yesterday about noon. Lester Johnson was here and keeping an eye on things, making sure the work was done right. They were about done, and I helped him load a couch he acquired into your new trailer. Took us a while to figure how to fit it through the door. If I were you, I'd break it into pieces before I'd try to get it out.

"Anyway, I mentioned your plight at the meeting, and we decided we wanted to help you. We've been all morning buying stuff we thought you'd need to start over. We'll start carrying things in. All you have to do is tell us where to put it. The ladies will set out a spread for lunch while we're doing that, and then we'll eat. Does that sound good?"

Roger felt dumbfounded. "I don't know what to say. I probably don't deserve this."

Pastor Nassey smiled. "You probably don't, but never say no to unexpected and undeserved providence, especially from God and His people."

Roger sniffed. "I can't believe you're doing this. Thank you so much." He wiped a tear from his eye.

Pastor Nassey turned to the group. "Okay, let Operation Bless Roger commence. It's show time. The sooner we're done, the sooner we can dive into the ladies' cooking, and you all know how Southern church women can cook."

Several heads nodded. Others smiled from ear to ear. The men and one stocky woman unloaded the furniture and heavy boxes from the trucks. They kept Roger busy pointing out where he wanted everything. If they'd forgotten anything, he couldn't figure out what it was. There were all kinds of foodstuffs: canned goods, boxed items, some frozen goods, milk, and a little produce and fruit. They'd even thought of pots and pans, dishes, cups, salt, pepper, and a few spices.

A full-size bed went in the larger bedroom. Bunk beds for the smaller bedroom. And they'd even thought of sheets, blankets, and pillows with cases. They left a box of clothes on the bed for Roger to go through later.

Just as they sat a box of bathroom supplies on the toilet, a woman with a very loud voice hollered, "Come and get it."

The trailer quickly emptied as everyone gathered around two large tables overflowing with food. They held hands as Pastor Nassey gave a brief prayer over the feast. Then they handed paper plates out along with napkins wrapped around eating utensils. Everyone got a gigantic piece of fried chicken. Sliced and pulled pork was available, along with buns and barbecue sauce. Of course, an iron kettle with baked beans tempted everyone, as did the Southern style potato salad. Cole slaw and fried okra rounded out the spread. A cooler filled with soft drinks and bottled water emptied quickly.

It didn't take long for the hungry crowd to devour much of the meal at the tables and folding chairs they'd brought along. Everyone made small talk after finishing. Roger conversed with one of the deacons who said he was a fifth generation Floridian. His family came as homesteaders before the Civil War. They originally landed in Philadelphia from Scotland and made their way south through several states farming and hunting along the way before ending up in Florida. Roger wondered if they might be relatives, but before he could find out, Pastor Nassey rose to speak.

"Folks, thank you for coming and helping us bless a man in great need, Roger Pyles. Few of us will ever go through a house fire losing everything. We're glad to be a part of helping him recover. It's said it's more blessed to give than receive. I believe one of the reasons for that is because if you have something to give, you've already been blessed. A poor man has little or nothing to give. We make our livings by what we get, but we make our lives by what we give. Roger, we hope this will help you on your road to recovery. And thank you ladies for the scrumptious meal. It's a wonder with all this fine food we're not as wide as we are tall."

Everyone clapped, and a few said, "Amen."

Pastor said, "I have a Bible for you, too. Everyone here signed it."

Roger rose and took the book. "I hardly know what to say. If the Last Supper'd had this much food, they'd never finished eatin'. I appreciate so much what you've done for me. Thank you all for everything."

Several tears rolled down his cheeks as they applauded. Then each got up and gave him a hug. After the last, Roger found his face flooded. He felt so loved.

The ladies cleaned up the tables but one and a few chairs. They placed the leftovers in some plastic containers. Roger could have them later. It didn't take long for everyone to pack up and be off. The only ones left were Roger and the pastor.

"Roger, you have a few minutes?"

"Sure, Pastor. You know I always can find time for you."

"Okay, grab a seat."

Roger laid the Bible on the table, found a chair left behind, and sat across from the pastor. "What's on your mind?"

"It's important. You see..."

Chapter 22

"Hey, wait a minute. Where's K9? In spite of all this commotion goin' on, I ain't seen her. Have you seen her? Where is she?" Roger said.

"No need to worry. She greeted us with a growl and some suspicion, but when she saw me, everything was okay. I stroked her head and reassured her we were no threat. A couple of pieces of pulled pork helped, too. She's not far. Didn't want to get trampled underfoot with this crowd," Pastor said.

"How about Donkey? Where's he?"

"He looked us over carefully, decided we were benign, and last time I saw him, was headed for the perimeter of your property. Your four-legged security systems did not fail you."

Roger said, "That's good to know. Had me worried a little." He paused. "Have you seen my cat?"

Pastor said, "I saw a streak that took off for the woods when we drove up. Didn't get a good look at it, but I think it was a cat."

"That sounds like her. Skittish and doesn't like strangers or crowds. I figured she was okay, but was still worried about her." He stopped and smiled. "I really want to thank you for doing this. You guys didn't have to. I could afford to do it myself, but you've saved me countless hours of time gettin' everything together. I don't know how to thank you."

"I believe you just did. We try to help where we can and who we can. This old world has a lot of needs."

"But why me? Of all the people in this world, why me? Why do all these rotten things happen to me? And occasionally, something good, like you guys blessing me. Why me?"

"I think you're asking a bigger question than what it appears."

Roger said, "I am. You know some of my background, how I unfairly lost my professor's job at the university and then my wife and son died in the auto accident. People have tried to kill me because I wanted to see justice done. Then I found out I have another son and then nearly lost him. My trailer's damaged and then burns up, but I did get out along with my critters. And now you guys help me? Why me?"

Pastor said, "You're asking a question people have asked for thousands of years, probably since the beginning of time. Have you considered Job?"

"I thought you might mention him."

"He wasn't doing anything wrong; fact is he was doing everything right, and that's what caused his problems and heartaches. Granted, we all suffer from outside influences. And some people suffer from their own actions and choices."

Roger nodded. "Yes, got to agree with you about some pain being self-inflicted because of bad personal choices and those of family members. But what about those who suffer for no reason at all? What about them? Good people that suffer from cancer and illness? Blindness? Mental health issues? Why do they have to suffer? Why?"

"That's a good question, Roger. This may come off as trite, but it's the only answer there is. We live in a fallen world where bad things happen to everyone. It rains on the good and bad. Too little rain and you get a drought, and people suffer. Too much rain and the

116

floods come, and people suffer. Even if you have just the right amount of rain, so the crops grow fine, people still suffer."

"That's not very uplifting, Pastor."

"No, it's not, but it's our reality. I could go into a long-winded explanation of how God is aware of it all and provides us comfort and a way through it all, but I know you've heard this from me before. Still the best answer I know for it is from the book of Job. This world is a mess. People suffer, good and bad, but God is always there and provides comfort. Sometimes straight from Him and sometimes He uses people in the process. That may not be the answer you want to hear, but it's the best one out there that I know of."

Roger sighed. "It's not fair."

"No, it's not, but it's the only answer we have." He stopped. "Fairness. Why should this world be fair? Where do we get that concept? I believe it comes from God, because we know in our hearts it's not fair, and there has to be something better."

They sat in silence for a while.

Roger said, "That's a lot to think about."

"Yes, it is. So, where do you go from here?"

"I don't know for sure. Your words are worthy of more consideration, and I have other fish to fry, like will I get another case to work on. I was all hepped up to investigate it and the rug got pulled out from under me when it was unexpectedly solved. I'm still trying to figure out my exact relationship with Gloria and our son, Carlos. I got a lot of things I could do. Some meaningful, some not. Some just to occupy time."

Pastor said, "Life can be like that. Sometimes it's desert. Sometime a rain forest. There's a time for every season under heaven. Ecclesiastes. Even the desert has its place. I don't know if you've ever seen the desert in bloom, but it's beautiful. Every one of those gnarly, thorny bushes and cactuses can put out the most beautiful of flower displays when conditions are right. There's a lot you can learn even when you go through a desert."

"Guess there is when you put it that way."

"A man has to have a reason to get up and something to do every day if life is to have meaning or he dies. I've seen that happen so many times when a person gets lost in life, whether it's depression or retirement. You have to have those two things for life to have meaning, or we die. Sometimes it's a little at a time. Sometimes it's pretty quick."

At that time, K9 came through an open space in the trailer skirting and sat at Roger's feet. She gave him a doggy smile and a little yelp.

"Good girl. Good old dependable K9. You always know when I need companionship." Roger stroked her head. "Good girl. I think you enjoy a head rub as much as I do."

"It's no wonder dogs are called man's best friend. They can be loyal to a fault."

"How right you are, Pastor. Thanks so much for all your help."

Pastor looked at his watch. "How time flies. I got to get over and visit old lady Tallman. She's on her last legs. Her time among the living is drawing to a close. She's lucky to have family to care for her."

"Yup, some family you can depend on. Some you can't."

"Going to have to agree with you there. I better be hitting the trail. Give me a call if you need anything more."

"I'll keep that in mind, Pastor. You have a great rest of your day. Thanks again."

"You're welcome. See you later."

The pastor walked to his car. Roger watched it disappear down Canaveral Flats Boulevard.

Roger stroked the hair on K9's head and back. "Well girl, I sure didn't see that coming. What a blessing. Wonder what else this day has waitin' for me? Desert or rain forest? Blessing or cursing? Will I see them for what they are? Katie bar the door. Damn the torpedoes. Guess it's full speed ahead for now. Keep on keepin' on."

Chapter 23

"Grrrr." K9 rose to her feet, looked toward Canaveral Flats Boulevard, and growled again, "Grrrr."

"What is it, K9?" Roger said. "What do you see?"

She growled again.

"I don't see nothin'."

Now he could hear a truck coming.

K9 growled again as a truck came into view.

"I should have known what was gettin' your knickers in a knot. Bill Kenney. Maybe we'll get lucky and he'll keep goin'."

But the Chief of Police stopped in front of Roger's place, opened the gate, and drove down the lane to Roger's trailer.

"K9, be a good girl and disappear under the trailer. I've warned you if you bite him, you'll regret it and never get the nasty taste out of your mouth, even if you eat something long dead and rotten."

Once more she growled, but she moseyed through the opening in the trailer skirting.

"Good girl."

Bill pulled up in front of the trailer, got out, and said, "Hey, Roger. How you doin'? Looks like you're moving up in the world.

Your new abode looks better than most of the housing in Canaveral Flats. Getting better? Are you doing okay?"

He grumbled under his breath, "I was until you showed up."

"What was that? Can't say I heard you. Got a little head cold and my ears are somewhat stopped up."

Roger said loudly, "I'm doin' alright, considerin' what I've been through."

"You don't have to yell. I have a stuffed-up head. I'm not deaf. Probably got something from you."

Roger grumbled, "Well, come on in. Let's hear what's on your mind."

"Some gratitude. You camp on my coach for four days sick as a dog, and this is the thanks I get? Lighten up."

Roger grimaced. "Sorry, still not feeling up to snuff."

"Hmmm. Sounds like the same grumpy old man I know."

"Hey, I said I was sorry and not feeling good." He paused, tried to smile, and said, "So, what's on your mind?"

"Just checking on you, Roger. You've had a lot to deal with lately, emotionally and physically. Your case got solved, the storm damaged your trailer, then it caught fire and burned up, and next you got sick, and here we are today with you in a new place. How is it?"

"Bigger and nicer than the old place. I got to thank Lester for overseeing the trailer set up and the new porch. I think I'm gonna like it."

Bill said, "Well, it wouldn't take much to be an improvement over that ancient, well-worn fire trap you had."

"You got me there." Roger shifted in his seat. "Yeah, friends have been lookin' out for me. Lester, Suzie, you, and others like Pastor Nassey."

"Pastor Nassey?"

"Yeah, he and a bunch of his church people were just here a little while ago, and blessed the daylights out of me."

"How so?"

"I had a completely empty trailer till they showed up with about every item known to man that you could ever use to set up a home. My refrigerator is full. They left furniture, bedding, and all kinds of stuff. I got blessed beyond my wildest dreams."

Bill said, "That sounds like something the Pastor and his gang would do. I've heard of other people in need in the area they've helped get back on their feet. They're a good bunch and they never go around bragging about what they've done."

"Well, they sure helped me, and I, for one, ain't gonna be bashful about talkin' about it."

Bill smiled. "Yeah, I think the word spreads faster when they're quiet and let others do the talking."

"Think you're right." Roger turned to Bill. "Did you say my other case had been solved?"

"Yeah, I did. They found the guy who killed the girl you found buried on your property across the road."

"How did they do that so quick?"

"That information you and Fred gave about the strange vehicle he saw late at night. The tag number was the key. We put a BOLO, be on the lookout for it, and a day later it got stopped in New Hampshire. The guy got in a shootout with the highway patrol up there. Guess he knew the law was after him and he chose to make a stand on a busy roadway up there. Fortunately, the cop had backup, and they were better shots than the criminal. And he had another dead girl in his trunk."

Roger said, "Sorry to hear about the other girl, but I'm glad he's been stopped, and I played a little part in it."

"A big part. The tag was the key. Thank you, Fred."

"Guess so, but I was hopin' to get the case and solve it. Bummer."

"You can't depend on getting cases and then solving them. That's not how this old world works."

"Guess so." Roger paused. "I must have had a terrible fever when I was sick on your coach."

"Suzy said you did. 102."

"I think I may have hallucinated."

"Oh."

"I dreamed I saw a naked man walkin' around your place. He even went to your cupboard, got a cookie, ate it, and then disappeared. What a nightmare." He stopped. "Weird, ain't it?"

"Well," Bill cleared his throat, "That may have been me. As you know, I sleep in the buff, and I have been known to sleepwalk."

"That's good to know. I was beginnin' to question my sanity."

Bill laughed, "We've all questioned your sanity, but for you, this time was a false alarm. But the other times-"

"Hey! You didn't have to agree with me so quickly."

Bill laughed again. "Just had to get you going, old buddy."

Roger growled, "Thanks, old buddy. You sure know how to make a fella feel good."

"Can I tell you a funny story that happened to me this week? It should make you feel better."

"Sure, old buddy. Lay it on me."

"Okay, here goes." Bill cleared his throat. "I got a call from one of the residents of our little town. He was all upset. It seemed his 15-year-old son had ran off with a Cocoa Beach stripper."

Roger's eyebrows went up. "Yeah, I can see how that would get your attention."

"I went right over and found him boo-oohing about his predicament. He handed me a letter his son had left, but he'd only read about half of it. He said he was too upset to read the rest."

"So, what did it say?"

"I'll repeat it best I can remember," Bill said.

He cleared his throat again. "Dear Dad, I'm sorry I have to tell you this, but I've eloped with my new girlfriend. I'm leaving this letter because I didn't want to make a scene with you and mom. I'm finding real passion with Lacy, at least that's the name she uses at the strip club. I know you don't approve of her piercings, tattoos, leather clothes, the fact she's much older than me, or all the money she makes at the club.

"You see, Dad, it's not only passion, she's pregnant. We'll live happily in her old trailer in the woods, and she wants to have more kids with me.

"Lacy's introduced me to weed and other drugs. We got lots of money from growing and selling it, too. We'll do alright.

"Let's hope they find a cure for AIDS so she can get better. She deserves it.

"No need to worry, Dad. I'm 15 and can take care of myself. We'll come to see you with the grandkids.

"Love to you and Mom, Donnie.

"P.S. Dad, ain't none of this true. I'm over at Ted's house. I had to remind you there's worst things in life than a rotten report card. You'll find it on the kitchen table under the place mat. Let me know when it's safe to come home. Donnie."

Bill continued. "After reading it to myself, I read the last part to the man who made the call. He sat there dumbfounded at first, then relieved, then angry, and finally he laughed and said, 'Don't that beat all? I was about to have a nervous breakdown, and it was all just a ruse to get me going. I'm not sure if I should punish him or give him a medal for creative thinking.'"

Roger said, "So what did you two work out?"

"He asked me what I thought he should do. I told him it was his problem and to work it out. I knew he would, and I also told him, no bloodshed. He nodded, and I left him sitting, considering his options. I've gotten no more calls, so I guess they worked it out."

"That's a pretty interesting story, and it does bring a smile to one's face."

Bill said, "I wish they all had a happy ending. I've seen some terrible things I wish I could unsee."

"I'll bet you have." Roger shifted in his chair. "So, how are you and my cousin Suzy getting along, still okay?"

"We're getting along just fine. We're both busy working, but we do go out for a movie and supper occasionally. She seems like a great gal."

"I'll ask again. You got feelings for her?"

"I do, and I believe it's mutual. Don't know if anything will develop further, but neither of us wants to cut it off at present."

Roger said, "You be good to her. She's been hurt, and I don't want to see anything bad happen to her."

"Why, Roger, I think you almost care. What's come over you?"

Roger gave Bill a dirty look. "Guess I'm getting soft in my old age, and she is family. I don't have much left, which leads me to doing something I wouldn't normally do."

"What's that?"

"Ask you for some advice."

A look of surprise showed on Bill's face. "You want advice from me? You must be desperate."

"Confused is more like it."

Bill said, "Okay, Mr. Confused. Tell Dear Abby about it."

Roger shifted in his seat. "It involves Gloria... and Carlos."

Bill nodded. "I see. Go on."

"My relationship with them is kinda confused. Gloria can be alright at times, but other times she can drive me nuts."

"So far, so good. Sounds like pretty normal male and female interactions for people with a history, as you two do."

"It's more than that. I stopped over at her place for lunch. We wanted to discuss how we could be raising Carlos separated and not married as we are. The wine she had was good and more potent than we realized, and we ended up in bed together. Seems like one thing we have in common is we enjoy sex together."

Bill said, "And you're giving me a hard time about my relationship with Suzy?"

"Ironic, ain't it? But you haven't heard the worst of it yet."

"Which is?"

"We fell asleep afterward, and Carlos came home from school and found us still there in bed together naked as jaybirds."

Bill stroked his chin. "I see. That must have been interesting, to say the least."

"Difficult and embarrassing it was for us. Carlos seemed to take it all in stride and went to his room. We collected our clothes, got dressed, and I left shortly afterward." Roger sighed. "So, I've got myself in another real pickle." He stopped. "Any idea what I should do next?"

Bill was quiet for a moment. "First off. Cut me some slack about Suzie."

"Point taken."

Bill cleared his throat. "You've got a lot of possibilities, and I'm sure you'll come up with something. After all, you are the great sleuth, Roger Pyles."

"Well, the great sleuth, Roger Pyles, is feelin' a little overwhelmed at this moment."

"I'm not surprised. The best advice I can give you is to chill, take a little break, get refreshed before you try to conquer all your problems and the worlds. Do what mothers do when little kids feel like you."

"What's that?"

"Have a snack - eat something, and take a nap - rest. Works every time. After that, you'll be better prepared to face life's challenges."

Roger said, "Sounds like good advice, but one thing keepin' me from doin' that?"

"And that is?"

"You. My cup is full and runneth over. I need a nap."

Bill smiled. "Okay, grouchy little kid. I'll go away, and you go take a nappy."

"That sounds good. And old buddy, thanks for hearin' me out and checkin' on me."

"Oh, I got one more thing, a housewarming gift I left in the truck. I'll get it."

Bill got up and quickly returned with something in a large paper sack. He handed it to Roger. "Enjoy."

Roger opened the bag and found two 6-packs of Yuengling beer. "Thanks. One beer should put me right off to sleep."

"I caught wind of how the church was going to bless you. It's hard to keep a secret in a small town. I didn't think they'd be getting beer for your refrigerator, so I got you some."

"And you'll probably just happen to stop in and end up drinkin' half of it."

Bill smiled. "That sounds about right. Maybe more."

"You want one right now?"

"I do, but I have to get back to work. This wellness visit is over. Got to go. Bye."

"Bye."

Bill waved from his truck, and it soon disappeared down Canaveral Flats Boulevard in a cloud of dust, as it was the dry season.

Roger felt a wet nose on his hand. "K9! Don't surprise me like that."

She ignored his protest and rubbed against his hand.

"K9, you make me feel wanted."

He rubbed her head and back for some time. It was hard to tell who was enjoying it more.

"Well, K9, Doctor Bill says I need a nap. I know it works for you. You guard the place from any nefarious types, okay, while I snooze in the trailer. Got to get me another La-Z-Boy for out here on the porch."

She gave an agreeable little yelp.

"I thought you'd say that. Now, off to lala land for me."

Roger got up, went inside, and laid down on the new bed. He thought about all that had happened to him recently. Yeah, he needed a break, but what to do? He drifted off to sleep with those thoughts in his mind. With some rest, he'd be ready to face his problems and a new day. His subconscious would be at work while he slept, and maybe, just maybe, he'd have some answers when he awoke.

Chapter 24

Roger's sleepy brain registered someone pounding on his door and yelling his name. His heart pounded as he rolled to the floor. Who was the offender, and what did he or them want? His heart skipped a beat. He snuck a peek through the lower corner of the curtainless window in his new bedroom. Gloria. It was not only Gloria, but Chief of Police Bill Kenney was with her. What did they want?

"Quit your poundin'. I'll be right there," he hollered. He grumbled to himself, "Some people can't let a man get a good night's sleep." What time is it? He looked at his watch. It said 12. Midnight or Noon? It was daylight outside. It had to be noon ... Noon? He'd slept till noon! He couldn't believe it.

Roger quickly dressed, went to the door, and opened it. "What's so important you guys are tryin' to tear my new door down? I thought some bad guys had found me and wanted to do me harm. Can't a guy get some sleep?"

Gloria gave him a look that could kill. Roger stepped back.

"Grrfff," came from her exasperated mouth. "Roger, I pounded and shouted for ten minutes! You could sleep through an earthquake."

"Don't know if there's ever been an earthquake in Florida. Hurricanes, yes. Earthquake, naw."

"Roger, I ought to kick your ass. I was concerned about you. Thought you were dead until I saw your chest moving. I thought maybe you'd had a stroke, so I called Bill Kenney."

"Bill, she's threatenin' me. You gonna allow that?"

"I may help her kick your ass if you don't shut up and listen to the lady."

Roger bit his tongue. *Lady. Who are you tryin' to fool?* Wisely, he kept his mouth shut until he found better words. "Okay, what brings you here today?"

Gloria said, "We need to talk."

Roger's stomach turned sour. If there were ever four words a man never wanted to hear from a woman, it was, "We need to talk." He was trapped. "Okay," he muttered. "Find a seat."

Bill said, "Gloria, you be okay with this madman?"

"If he gives me any trouble, I'll kick his sorry ass all the way down Canaveral Flats Boulevard to US 1."

"Okay, if you need any assistance with that, just call, and I'll come running."

"I'll remember that, but I think I can handle Roger."

Roger smiled and said nothing.

Bill said, "Okay, I'll be off, but let me know if you need me."

She nodded, and Bill got in his truck and drove off.

She said, "I've been trying to reach you since I heard about the fire, but nothing worked."

Roger said, "Yeah, chaos has reigned supreme in my life recently. First, the windstorm blew a tree on the trailer that ruined it. Then it caught fire and burned up the next night. And then I got sick and ended up squatting on Bill's couch for four days. It's been a long time since I've been that sick. I still haven't gotten over it completely. It just keeps hangin' on. That why I was still dead to the world at noon and didn't hear you makin' all the racket tryin' to get my attention. How you like my trailer?"

"Much better than the last one."

"And now you hit me with this, we need to talk."

She shifted in her seat. "You've been through a lot."

"I have, but what's on your mind? I need to make a trip to town. Get a new La-Z-Boy chair, some curtains, and some other stuff like a phone. Tell me what's on your mind."

"About our lunch time activities." She stopped. "This is difficult. After you left, I had a little talk with Carlos. I told him sometimes adults do some things that may embarrass kids his age, and besides, we were his father and mother."

"I wondered how you were gonna explain it to him. How did he take it?"

"All in stride. Didn't seem to faze him at all. That boy is mentally years ahead of his actual age."

Roger nodded. "No argument on the last part. Where's that leave us now?"

"Roger, you're a great guy. I don't know if we could ever make it happen."

"Like a real family?"

"Yeah. But it seems like what we have in common is when we get drunk together, we end up in bed together, and that's not the right key to a marriage. You must think I lured you over, then got you drunk, and tried to hook you with sex. Honestly, I didn't know that wine was so potent."

Roger said, "I believe you. It could happen and has before." He paused. "Now, where do we go from here?"

"I don't know. Roger, that's the first time I had sex since I was with you in Vegas, and we ended up making Carlos."

"First time for me since my wife died." He sighed. "Yeah, it was good, but I don't want to make a habit of it. If I want a lover, I want it to be my spouse."

Gloria nodded. "Same here. Trust me. It's a lot less trouble and safer."

"Yeah. So, where do we go from here? I guess we just keep muddling along until we can get an idea of what to do. You got any other better ideas on this matter?"

She shook her head. "No," she said and sighed. "No, I don't."

They sat in silence for some time. Roger shifted. "I need to get to town. Is there anything more you need to speak with me about?"

She planted her palm on her forehead and swore. "I almost forgot. We were so involved with our own relational problems, I nearly left without telling you."

"Tellin' me what."

"Some bad news. ODESSA, that Nazi organization, has surfaced and is on the move. We got a notice from the FBI to be on higher alert concerning them. There are no known plots going on, but the fact they are still around is concerning."

Roger said. "Yeah, you got that right. Thanks for the warning."

"I would have told you early if there was a way, but I needed to talk to you face to face about us."

"How is Carlos, our son?"

"He wants to see you."

"Good, I want to see him. Say, just curious, how much longer is your lease on the apartment?"

"About a month and a half. Landlord wants to raise my rent substantially. I got to give him a yea or nay by the end of the month."

Roger asked, "Did you see that big pile of dirt across the road?"

"Yeah, how could I miss it?"

"That's my property, and I was thinkin' about puttin' a double-wide modular home on it. Three bedrooms, two baths. Would you be interested?"

"How much?"

Quickly, he figured a price he felt they could both live with and told her.

"I'll take it. Can you have it done in a month?" She said.

"Sure. Let's shake on it."

She put her hand forward, and they did. "Cop's honor."

"Yup," he said. "Cop's honor."

"Roger, I'd like to talk some more, but duty calls. I need to be in the office soon and I better go."

"That's fine. I should have a landline phone of some sort no later than tomorrow or the next day. You know how the phone company operates. It'll be the same numbers, so we can keep in touch."

"That's great. Got to go. Bye."

Roger watched the rise and fall of her hips as she ran to her vehicle. Lusty thought came to his mind, and he smiled.

She caught his eye as she drove off and returned his smile and waved. Roger returned her gesture. Her vehicle disappeared down the road to US 1. Now he had to get to town. He had a lot to do. How was he going to get the new place up and ready for Gloria and Carlos in just a month? A plan slowly formed in his mind. Yeah, he just might be able to pull this off with a little luck and everything going his way. A lot could go wrong, and he didn't want to have to face the wrath of Gloria. It better work. He'd find a way or die trying.

Chapter 25

Roger drove down US 1 to the La-Z-Boy store. He made good time, as traffic was light. He saw a new sign for a development that advertised luxury homes at affordable prices and wondered how it would affect road congestion. Not good for sure, but there was little he could do about it. Like trying to hold back the tide or time.

The salesman recognized him and was curious about him buying another, his third chair. Why, he must really love the chairs. Roger told him how the first got shot up, the second burned up, and now he needed a third, which he hoped would last a long time. The salesman laughed and told him of a Wyoming game warden who kept getting his truck destroyed in the line of duty one way or the other. He was on his fourth truck in four years, and the state wasn't happy. Trouble seemed to follow him. Roger said he understood completely and chuckled at the man's misfortune.

The salesman said he'd deliver it today. He remembered Roger's old place. Roger told him of the new trailer, but put it on the porch if he wasn't there. Roger paid with a check, and a handshake finished the deal.

He drove on down to Merritt Island and stopped at Kmart across from Merritt Square Mall. He wanted to buy some pre-made curtains, but found the selection was daunting and nothing looked like it was the right size anyway.

He sighed. "Wish I'd measured the window size. Why does it have to be so complicated?" He realized there was a lot he didn't know, so he bought some extra sheets for the bed. He knew its size, and the sheets would work as curtains until he could get the real things that were the right size. His wife had always done this.

"Roger."

He turned to see who'd called his name and saw a short, older lady standing nearby. "Eva, what brings you here? Good to see you."

"Some shopping and some important business. By the way, it involved you, but I can't talk about it now."

He sensed urgency in her voice. "My day's pretty open, and I was heading home soon. I can meet you some place."

"How about the Black Cat Café in Port St. John by the Winn Dixie in about an hour?"

"That would work just fine. I'll see you then."

"I look forward to it. See you there. Bye."

Roger said bye and took his new sheets to the checkout and paid. On the way home, he stopped and got a gopher turtle out of the road. The chicken wasn't crossing the road, but the turtle was trying. Fortunately, he or she hadn't been hit by several cars that passed the reptile, as Roger waited for a safe time to rescue the creature. He hoped he hadn't hurt the turtle's feelings by not calling him or her the right gender, but he wasn't sure about turtle sexing. He hoped the turtle didn't care as long as he was safe from traffic, but the turtle didn't seem to appreciate his effort. He hissed at Roger as he picked him up off the road. Surprised, he almost dropped him, but managed to hold on until he could release the turtle in the bushes along the side of the road.   "Good bye, Turtle. Find you way back home, no more dangerous crossings of the highway." It didn't seem to sink in. He wished he could speak turtle, or the turtle knew English. With his recent luck, he'd found a turtle that only spoke Spanish.

His good deed done, he drove north and turned into the Winn Dixie Shopping Center parking lot. He grabbed several items at the supermarket, placed them in his truck, and went to the café. Eva sat at a booth.

Roger said, "I hope I haven't kept you waitin' long."

She replied. "No, I just got here. I put in my order, sat down, and in you came. Get what you want and then we'll talk. I have much to tell you."

"Okay." Roger did as he was told. He ordered a large black coffee and a tuna salad sandwich. The barista told him to expect it in five minutes or less. He paid and sat across from Eva.

"It's good to see you," he said. "I trust all is well with you."

"My health has been good. I've managed to not catch the nasty bug that's going around. Knock on wood." She rapped her knuckles on the table. "Old Jewish superstition for good luck."

Roger laughed. "Must have been a lot of Jews in my hometown in the Appalachians. Lots of people there do the same. Wished I'd been so lucky. I've been sick, and my old trailer was damaged beyond repair, caught fire, and burned down. Fortunately, with a little help from my friends, I now have a new, better trailer, and I'm on the mend."

She said, "A true friend is one you can depend on."

"So, why did you need to talk to me? What's goin' on?"

She shifted uncomfortably in her seat, open her mouth to speak, when the barista appeared with their orders. He placed them on the table in front of them. "Enjoy. Let me know if you need anything more."

Roger said, "Okay." Eva nodded in agreement.

The young man left.

Roger sipped his coffee. "Very good. Everything's good here."

Eva said, "The menu's a little limited, but everything I've ever tried had surpassed my expectations." She sipped her coffee and looked Roger directly in the eyes. "I have bad news. ODESSA has reappeared."

"A deputy told me they'd received concerning information about that Nazi group. So, it's more than just underworld chatter?"

"Unfortunately, yes. Rabbi Katz is a friend. I was over at his office, and he filled me in on a few of the details. No one seemed to know what they're up to or if they're a credible threat of some sort of trouble, but they have reared their ugly head. A synagogue in Chile was recently bombed. No one claimed responsibility. Local police have been close lipped about it, but it has all the markings of an ODESSA operation. And a Lutheran church in the same country suffered a similar fate. Many of the people in the congregation were Germans who fled the Nazis. Five people died in the latter incident."

Roger swallowed his bite of sandwich. "That's not good. Anything local happenin' I should know about?"

She said, "Some reports of gun and drug running in Mexico, but only rumors of rumors in the US. Still, Rabbi Katz advised me we should be on heightened alert."

"That would sound prudent."

"Evil is never far away, and it seems to want our children, the most vulnerable. If it can't twist their minds, it seeks to destroy them. The rabbi told me a story of two girls born before the war in Poland. Neither knew their birthdate. One was abandoned on the steps of a church, and the other was raised by nuns. An older brother somehow managed to find them after many years of searching. They were all Jews. He'd joined the Polish underground, been wounded, but managed to survive the war. It was his quest to find his sisters. His parents, grandparents, and a brother died in the concentration camps."

She paused, took a sip of coffee, and said, "Roger, can you imagine how frightened a mother must be to abandon her children? The story of Moses comes to mind. Pharaoh wanted to kill all the Hebrew male babies. Herod had all the little boys in Bethlehem slaughtered to try to get Jesus.

"These people and others with similar types of ideologies, whether it's secular or religious, hate us and want to impose their ideas on us, as if we, in their eyes, are too dumb or get in the way, we must be eliminated. Like many religious zealots, they see themselves in an epic struggle to overcome us for the good of a better world filled with their twisted ways they want to create. They think of others as evil when in truth, they represent the head of the beast that seeks to devour our children, families, and society."

She shifted in her seat and moved closer to him. "Roger, the only people I know who oppose evil like this are Christians and Jews. Common criminals know what they're doing is wrong, but the most dangerous ideological movements, like atheist communism, fascism, and other like-minded groups that have killed tens of millions, rarely believe they're in the wrong, but on the right side of history. These people hate us, and we must defend ourselves and our families from them."

Roger nodded. "A knight is not a knight without his weapon."

"Have you read any Tolkien?"

"I've read the Lord of the Rings trilogy."

"Good," she said. "In The Two Towers, Aragon said, 'I do not love the bright sword for its sharpness, nor the arrow for its swiftness, nor the warrior for his glory. I love only that which they defend.'" She stopped. "Roger, I believe it's our duty and responsibility to protect others and those we love. First, we must try to persuade those who disagree with us that we don't hate them and that our cause is just. If they disagree and leave us alone, fine. Most

140

people just want to live their lives and be left alone. But if they try to harm the innocent or defenseless, we need to stop them."

Roger said, "Them's some powerful, fightin' words."

"I know. Evil's contained in the human heart, and until we can control and change that, I'm afraid we'll have to fight it again and again. I've seen evil and know if it's not stopped early, then it rolls over good people, and leaves death and destruction in its path. Love means telling evil it's wrong in hopes it will see the light and change course, but love is also defending the good there is and fighting evil until it's vanquished."

They sat in silence for a few moments and sipped their coffee.

Eva spoke, "Roger, sorry if I got on my soapbox, but this matter is dear to my heart, and, as you can tell, I feel strongly about it."

Roger nodded. "I'm glad you got it out. I couldn't have stated it any better and will remember this talk as long as I live. In a nutshell, you said we should love our neighbor, but we may need to use actual force to defend the innocent and defenseless from those who want to kill and maim them."

"Yes, I don't know all that's ahead of us, but I know human history, and we need to be on guard. There's evil in this world, and it often pretends to be what's right and good. We must nip it in the bud, and if worse comes to worse, cut down the whole tree and burn it till only the ashes remain."

"Eva, I'm gonna have to go. Thank you for tellin' me all this. It made good sense. I have a lot to think about."

They both got up and left the café. As Roger drove down the road, a shiver went down his spine as he considered the possibilities of what could be ahead. He said a little prayer and hoped for the best.

Chapter 26

Roger pulled up to Lester's house and got out of his truck.

"Lester, I need help."

The old black man sat on the porch. He smiled. "I've known that for a long time."

Roger grimaced. "This goes beyond the normal. I've got a problem, and I know you're the one who I can trust to getterdun."

"And what would that be?"

"First off, let me thank you so much for seein' my new trailer got set up right. I walked in, and everything worked. The lights. The plumbing. The blocks underneath. Everything."

Lester said, "Did you notice the tie downs? I had the best available added and installed. No point in getting a new trailer and a windstorm or hurricane blowing it over."

"Yeah, I saw that. What did it cost you?"

"Nothin'. You'll get the bill from the trailer setup people. I knew you'd need it and want it. There'll be more storms in this life."

"Tell me about it. You would know, and I'm learning."

Lester asked, "So, what's the current emergency?"

"You know all about me buyin' the old Flanagan place across the street from my place."

"I do. I saw all the dirt you added to raise it up. What you gonna do with it now?"

Roger said, "I want to put a double-wide on it, and I need it livable ASAP, in less than a month."

"That's not much time."

"I know. That's why I came to you. I knew if anyone could getterdun, it was you. You know all the right places and people. I need it done quickly or I'm in a lot of hurt."

Lester smiled. "What kind of in-a-bind have you got yourself into this time?"

"I sort of promised Gloria I'd have her a place to move into in less than a month. Her rental agreement is up at the end of the next month, and she needs a place to stay."

"That would make it more convenient for you to see your son."

"Yeah, and she'd have cheaper rent, too."

Lester shifted in his old beat-up chair. "So, you over-committed yourself, and now you want me to save your skin from the wrath of Gloria. She does seem to have a temper."

"She does, especially when people promise her something and then don't follow through. Can you do it?"

"I can, but do I want to? I haven't been formally asked."

Roger's face dropped. "Please, pretty please with a cherry on top."

Lester was quiet for a moment, and then he smiled. "Of course, I'll do it. You're not the first sorry creature I had to help or bail out."

"Thank you, thank you. I knew Lester wouldn't let me down."

"First off, I had to see how desperate you were, and then I'd make you beg a little before I'd consent to what I'd already decided in my mind I'd do."

Roger said, "Why, you scallywag. I should have known I was bein' played."

"So, do you want it done or not?"

"Of course, I want it done."

Lester asked, "What kind of double-wide?"

"A well-built one. Three bedrooms, two baths. 1000 to 1200 square feet set up ready to move in."

"That's about what I thought you'd want, but it'll cost you."

Roger said, "I thought so. My credit's still good with you?"

"It is, and I know where you live."

"Pick out a good one from the dealer, and have it installed. Either you can get some guys to do it, or have the dealer set it up."

Lester said, "I'll do the first. Got some friends that owe me some favors and could use the money."

"Sounds like we have a deal."

A noise inside the old house caused Roger to turn. "Lester, is Ruth here?" He smiled.

"No, my daughter's busy with work at this time. I got a guest, a friend of mine I met at the VFW."

Roger asked, "Male or female?"

"Male. He moved down here from Wyoming about six months ago."

"Wyoming. That's a beautiful state, but windy and cold."

Lester nodded. "That's what he said. He was tired of freezing his patootie off."

"Patootie. Did your military buddy really say patootie?"

"Well, it was a little stronger and colorful, but-"

"Lester, you didn't tell me you had friends in Hollywood." He stuck out his hand to Roger. "Why, Mr. Sam Elliott, what brings you here?"

Roger laughed. "I'm not Sam Elliott, though I get mistaken for him on a regular basis. It's led to some interestin' situations, if you get my drift." Roger took his hand and shook it. "Name's Roger Pyles. I'm just a country boy from a holler up in the Appalachians. I grew up in wild and wonderful West Virginia. Your name is...?"

"My name's Wayne Ferguson. Good to meet you, Mr. Ell..., I mean, Mr. Pyles." He let go of Roger's hand. "You sure you're not Sam Elliott? You even sound like him."

Lester spoke, "I know he could be Elliott's stunt double, but his name really is Roger Pyles. He's lived down here for, oh, two-three years now. He's a member of our community police force and also is on call with several local and state law enforcement groups."

Roger grunted. "Yeah, I'm an SOB, Special Operations Branch."

"SOB?" Wayne asked.

"Yeah, SOB. Beats the other thing they wanted to call the group," Roger said.

Wayne said, "What was that?"

"Special Homicide Investigations Team."

Wayne thought for a moment. "Why, that's SHI..." He laughed and slapped his knee. "I can see why you preferred the first."

Lester nodded. "We thought so, too. I hear there really is a police group with that moniker on the Pacific Coast in Seattle."

Wayne said, "Not surprising. Never did see a city on the West Coast I like, except maybe San Diego. Give me the wide-open spaces."

Lester said, "Like he said, we met at the VFW. Everyone there has some interesting war stories, but his is one of the best. Why don't you tell him, Wayne?"

"He don't wanna hear no old war stories from me."

Roger said, "Yes, I do. My dad was in the European Theater durin' World War II, but he passed some time ago. He didn't like to talk about it, but occasionally he would. It was difficult for him. Brought up old memories he'd like to forget. But sometimes he'd renege. He said we needed to know what happened and how bad it was. Maybe we'd learn and do better." Roger paused. "Please, tell me your story. It'll help bring back memories of my dad."

Wayne hesitated. "Okay." He sighed. "Brings up some horrible memories for me, too. Not sure how much I can bring up memories of your dad. I served in the Pacific, the Philippines, to be specific. You still want to hear it?"

"I do."

"In that case, it started a long time ago. I grew up on a ranch five miles from the nearest public road. Little did I realize the skills I learned there would keep me alive years later." He stopped. "You want the short version or the long?"

Roger said. "The long. I got the time, and I could use a good story."

Wayne smiled. "Okay, young fella, not Sam Elliott, but Roger Pyles. Here goes. I was born in the dead of winter during a howling blizzard in the Cowboy State. I was delivered by my grandmother and am the youngest of six children. My parents home

146

schooled us on that ranch in the middle of nowhere in central Wyoming. It was more than enough to get me into the University of Wyoming, and that's where the story gets interesting."

Chapter 27

"You have to realize I had no idea what I wanted to do at the university in Laramie," Wayne said. "Fortunately, I got an advisor who recognized my quandary and had me take a battery of tests. Turned out, I was good at math, and he suggested an engineering degree. I thought civil engineering would work, so while at the college, I got one of those degrees with the help of ROTC and found a wife who was the love of my life. God rest her soul."

He cleared his throat. "You sure you want the full story?"

Roger said, "Lay it on me."

"Okay, you asked for it. Now, where was I before I so rudely interrupted myself?"

Lester said, "Finished college, Army, and wife."

"Thank you," Wayne said, "The Army sent me to the Philippines, which at that time was American-administrated. My enlisted time went quickly and soon I was a civilian, but still in the Reserves. I continued working for the Army in the same position on the southern island of Mindanao, and along the way, became the father of three children.

"I was called to active service when the Japs invaded the Philippines. The Army evacuated civilians, women, and children. When the Army surrendered the island, I refused to do so. I'd developed a fondness for the people of the Philippines, and with my knowledge, helped organize them into an effective guerrilla army when asked to do so by several of their leaders. I promoted myself to brigadier general to gain respect from the guerrillas, but this irritated MacArthur and his staff to no end, I later found out. The natives hated the enemy because of their atrocities. One in every twenty Filipinos died during the war. We conducted hit-and-run raids on the enemy, and passed on vital information of Japanese Naval activities to US forces. We did every damned thing but surrender. I couldn't envision failure. I knew the odds were against us, and there was no way we could win with conventional warfare. If we only won part of the time and gained a little each time, in the end we would succeed.

"Eventually, we were able to get a few supplies from America forces. Some of MacArthur's staff were our biggest enemies. They thought sending arms, ammo, and supplies was a waste of resources. The Japs had defeated the regular US Army. What damage could a rag-tag bunch of under-equipped, poorly trained, and often barefoot band of irregulars do to better equipped and supplied Japanese troops? We showed them. We became a thorn in their flesh, ever present and irritating. The Japs were only able to control the cities on the coast where their bases were. We controlled the rest of the island. Sometimes we'd get lucky and sink an enemy ship. Filipino bolos took care of the survivors."

"Bolos? What's a bolo?" Roger said.

"Think of it like a razor-sharp machete slightly curved and wider near the end. The Filipinos exacted terrible retributions for the Japanese atrocities done during years of their occupation."

"Ouch," Roger said.

Wayne nodded. "Big ouch. Big deadly ouch." He stopped. "Still want to hear more?"

"Sure."

"It was difficult. At first, we had to depend on ourselves, and on whatever we had available. Eventually, we had to convince our own military to help us. We improvised wherever we could at first, even making alcohol from coconut palms as a gas substitute to run

149

our gasoline vehicle. We even had to make our own ammunition. I found I couldn't depend on some of the men surrounding me and had to send them elsewhere. And there were those in MacArthur's circle who still didn't like me or my methods. We did what we felt was right. We did what we had to do. Damn the naysayers.

"We were able to establish regular contact with the Navy, and they delivered much needed supplies, often 100 tons at a time via submarine, usually the USS Narwhal. The sub also evacuated guerrillas needing critical medical help and Americas who hadn't got out, mainly women and children. With regular supplies, the 30,000 or so men I commanded got more organized and made the Japs pay dearly. Sources say we killed 7,000 Japs and drained their resources. We tied up 60,000 of their troops they badly needed elsewhere chasing us around the island. We even built an airstrip US forces used to reconquer the island. More than anything else, we were able to keep up the morale and fighting spirit of the Filipinos. We believed we could do it, and they did, too.

"Got a little more. Are you still with me, Roger?"

"I'm all ears. Please continue."

"After the war, I was one of three men who helped establish the principles behind the Special Forces, our nation's unconventional warfare soldiers. And the Filipinos sure liked me. About 12 years after the war, the wife and me went back. I couldn't believe the people who greeted us. There were thousands singing and shouting, all dressed in their best clothes and uniforms. That made all the blood and guts I saw worth it. Do good. And you'll be thanked and rewarded in time.

"Roger, you can only depend on your own two hands and yourself. If you want something to happen, you need to make it happen. True friends will be there when you need them and need their help. Okay, I'm done. Did I wear out your ears?"

"No, I thoroughly enjoyed your story. It was incredible."

"You think my story was incredible? You ought to hear my friend Chase Mason's tale. His job during the war was to track Japanese fire balloons on horseback across our western states. All it took was one balloon to set hundreds of thousands of acres of forest on fire. He worked with the Triple Nickels. Lester, ever heard of them?"

"Can't say I have. Who are they?"

"Were. They were disbanded in 1950 like so many groups that took part in the war."

Roger said, "I never heard of them either. Who were they?"

"They were an all-black airborne unit in the Army formed in early 1944. Originally, they were supposed to be sent to Europe to reinforce battered Airborne units there, but were deployed to the West Coast. They thought they were going to fight the Japs on the Pacific Islands, but instead they ended up fighting them on the fire line in the Western United States in 1945. They became paratroopers and were used as smokejumpers. That's how Chase met them."

Lester said, "Sounds interesting. I doubt if we'll ever hear it firsthand if he's in Wyoming."

Wayne said, "He's supposed to come down for a visit in the near future. I'll let you know, and we can get together. And you can depend on it."

The men laughed.

Roger looked at his watch. "My, how time flies when you're havin' fun. I got to go. Thank you, Lester, for your promised help. You're a true friend." He turned to Wayne. "And thank you for that riveting story. I needed to hear it more than you needed to tell it. Thanks. Guys, I have to run. I'll see you all later."

Both Wayne and Lester said "Bye," almost simultaneously.

Roger drove down the washboard road known as Canaveral Flats Boulevard toward his new trailer. Things may just work out, but he wondered what difficulties lay ahead. He knew there were going to be some. That was for sure, but he felt confident he could meet them. Just give it your best and improvise.

Chapter 28

As Roger rolled up to his place, he saw his gate was open. He swore under his breath as he saw Donkey loping away down the road. *Oh no, Donkey's out for adventure.* He swore again.

There wasn't much he could do but follow him. Donkey zigged and zagged down the streets in the hinder parts of the town and stopped in the yard of an old house to eat some flowers. Roger shook his head and mumbled under his breath, "I should have known where he was headed, Mrs. Tallman's. Wonder what it's gonna cost me this time for flower damages?"

He walked to Donkey, who continued to eat more flowers. A small horse came from around the back of the house, stood next to Donkey, and also started to consume the flowers.

"Well, little fella. Where'd you come from? Are you an escapee, too? You look cared for. Is someone lookin' for you?"

He heard the door to the home open. A middle-aged, flat-chested woman looked at him.

She said, "I wondered when the cops were going to show up."

Roger thought she looked familiar, but he couldn't place her. He smiled and said, "Guess you know what I'm here for."

"Are you going to arrest me, Roger?" She could tell from his look he was bewildered.

"Why? My donkey is eatin' your flowers? Is this about the little horse?"

"You really don't recognize me, do you? Have I changed that much?"

Roger took a step back. "Who are you?"

"Peggy Sue Tallman. I last saw you on a beach in Baja, Mexico."

Roger's face dropped even lower. "I don't believe it. I thought you were..."

"Dead? No, I'm very much alive, for now. Are you going to arrest me? I am the notorious bank robber Cowboy Gene."

"Are you packin?"

"No." She pulled up her sundress, revealing her bare thighs where she'd carried a gun during their encounter in Mexico. "There's a gun in the house in a small safe. This is Florida, you know. You're safe here. I mean you no harm."

Roger said nothing for a moment.

"Cat got your tongue?" She asked.

"I don't know what to say."

"Then let's sit down on those two chairs in the shade." She pointed to two nearby.

"Okay, but what about your flowers?"

She said, "Don't worry about them. Looks like they're making two of God's critters happy. Let's sit and talk. I'll explain, and I have some questions for you, too."

Roger took a seat, as did Peggy Sue. He said, "Why did you come back? It must have been awful important for you to blow your cover. Everyone thinks you're dead. I thought you'd walked into the

Pacific and ended it all. I wasn't 100% sure, but I hoped I'd never see you again. You've put me in a conundrum."

"Yeah. Expect I have. Turn me in or not. She sighed. "The reason I came back was to care for my mother. She's on her last legs. The cancer will take her soon. She'd be in constant pain if it wasn't for the heavy meds."

"Where's your sister? Why isn't she takin' care of her?"

"My sister's in hospice. She's in worse shape than mom. She can't even talk. Family curse, cancer."

Roger was silent for a moment. "Why..."

"Why do I come back at all? To care for mom. My sister and I always looked a lot alike. People often got us confused. And this time, Roger, I really am dying. Cancer. Doctors give me six months to a year at best. I can show you the doctor's report if you want to see it."

Roger said nothing.

Peggy Sue said, "I know what you're thinking. If you turn me in, mom won't have a loving family member to care for her in her last days, or do you turn me in, and I spend my last days in prison being treated and housed at the Florida taxpayers' expense? It's your call."

Roger thought for some time. He cleared his throat. "What happened on the beach in Baja when I confronted you about your past? I didn't see you anywhere. I thought you'd walked into the water never to return, but I didn't see your dress floating anywhere."

"I hid behind some rocks. I watched you leave. After an hour or so when you didn't return, I knew you'd left. Your car wasn't in the parking lot. I breathed a sigh of relief. I lied to you about the cancer back then, but not now. I really am dying. I hoped I'd never see you again, but here we are. Whatever you choose, I won't hold it against you. Do what you think's best."

Roger said nothing as he thought about his predicament. "Is that your little horse?"

"No. He just showed up today. I hoped he'd find his way home, but he hasn't. Is he yours?"

"No. The reason I came here was my donkey got out and came here."

She said, "What are you going to do, Mr. Lawman?"

"Think I'm gonna take my ass home. I'll tie him to my truck and slowly walk him there. I hope the little horse will follow. You don't need him drawing attention here to you."

"Thank you, Roger, for looking the other way."

"I was never here. This never happened. Understand?"

She nodded, said nothing, and went into the house. Roger put a rope on Donkey and slowly drove off. The little horse followed along. At the slow pace, it seemed like it took forever to get home, but Roger passed no one on the drive home. Once there, he closed the gate and released Donkey. "Well, old boy. Looks like you found a friend. Now, what do we do with him?"

Donkey answered with cooing sounds.

Roger said, "That's easy for you to say. Wish I understood donkey."

Roger's life had just gotten more complicated. The little horse was a minor problem. Something would work out, but what about Peggy Sue? Had he done the right thing? What was the right thing? Sometimes what's legal may not be moral or just. As he contemplated his problems, Bill Kenney drove up and stopped.

Roger muttered under his breath, "Just what I need. More complications."

Chapter 29

Canaveral Flat's Chief of Police Bill Kenney got out of his truck and walked to the fence. He yelled, "Looks like you got 'em."

Roger gave Bill a thumbs up and went to the fence. "Yeah, I did. Had a little help from Donkey."

"I got a bunch of calls about a little horse running through the streets of our town. At first, I thought it was just a prank call. We get a bunch of them, but it turned out to be correct. I tried to catch him, but he was more slippery than an eel."

"That and he could run faster than you."

"I'm thinking about taking him in for resisting arrest. I chased him for two hours before I got a real call from somebody that needed help. I may just add trespassing to the growing list of charges."

"Now, Bill, how can you charge anythin' that cute with criminal offenses? Arrest a horse? Canaveral Flats will be the laughingstock of Brevard County."

"I think we already are. We're the Bithlo of Brevard. Which reminds me of a story about a governor of Pennsylvania sending a dog to prison, but that's another story and can wait until later." He paused. "How'd you catch him?"

Roger said, "It goes like this. I came home, and the gate was open. I saw Donkey headin' east toward US 1. Fortunately, he zigged and zagged through the back streets of Canaveral Flats. I found him eatin' Mrs. Tallman's flowers and the little horse was with him. I tied Donkey to my truck, came home, and the little horse came too."

"At Mrs. Tallman's. I see. So, like a good cop, you corralled him, and he's now in protective custody?"

"That pretty much sums it up. What are we gonna do with him?"

Bill said, "That's the sixty-four-dollar question. I called around, and nobody seems to be missing him. Animal Control can't take him. They handle cats and dogs, small animals. Told me to put him down, and none of the private animal shelters take horses."

"That's a shame. He's such a handsome little devil. Don't seem right."

"A little devil alright. Think I lost five pounds chasing him around. Hey, why don't you keep him till we can find a home for him?"

Roger said, "But you told me the same thing when I took Donkey. That was months ago, and he's still here."

"It should be easier for him. As you pointed out, he is a cute little rascal, and you got enough pasture for both of them. You're all set up for taking care of equestrians, and Donkey likes him."

"They do seem to get along, but this has to be temporary. When it gets dry, I barely have enough pasture for Donkey, even with the property I bought." He paused. "Okay, he can stay, but it has to be temporary. I don't want him put down."

Bill said, "Yeah, I'm not sure I could, either. One glance from those cute little sad eyes, and your heart melts."

"I know."

"Let me check around. There are a couple of therapy groups in the area that use horses. They might need and be willing to take a little guy like him. What're you going to name him?"

Roger grunted. "I know that trick, Bill. I name him, and he's mine. No, I'm just gonna call him LH, little horse, for now, and you're gonna find him a home. And that's final."

Bill smiled. "That's fair enough. Oh, there is one more thing I need to mention. I hear by way of the grapevine something could be going on with ODESSA. That's not good."

"Yeah, I've heard that from several sources. They said so far, it's all chatter. Nothing definite or concrete, but thanks for the information. I'll be on heightened awareness."

"Good. Got to go. Bye."

Roger watched as Bill's truck disappeared down the road. What had he gotten himself into this time? Another horse. He wondered if Bill would really try to find LH a home. And what about all these ODESSA rumblings? He felt a chill go up his spine in spite of the Florida heat. Evil was on the move, and he could be in its crosshairs. You could stomp it down, but it always seemed to show up again. He'd better be prepared for what could be coming.

Chapter 30

"Mrs. Smith, I'm coming in."

She growled, "Thanks for the warning, my dirty old man, husband," and she heard the bathroom door open and close. "Last time you did that, it didn't go well for you."

"Man, the steam's so thick in here, you could cut it with a knife. Wow."

"Are you wowing at the steam or my naked body?"

"The steam, of course."

"That's good," she said. "I've got shampoo in my hair, and it wouldn't be good for you if I got it in my eyes."

"Let me know when it's safe to enter your shower with you. No point in me being a dirty old man when I can get scrubbed up with you."

"You just stay out there, Mr. Smith, till I say you can come in."

He moaned. "Oh, very well."

"You remember what happened last time?" She could hear his eyes roll.

"How could I forget? What a mixture of pain and pleasure. Nothing like having a naked, mad woman on top of me."

She said, "Be glad I was only trying to stop the possible threat, not neutralize it."

"You nearly neutered me in the process."

"You recovered."

"Yes, I did." She could hear his smile. "I learned to be more careful with you, but it was a hard lesson."

She laughed. "Ruined your love life for a while." She paused. "Mine, too." She could hear him snicker as she rinsed the last of the soap and shampoo from her body. "Now, what's so important for you to risk physical injury? What do you have to tell me?"

He said, "I heard from the agency."

"Really? That's a surprise after you voiced your concerns."

"It's about unfinished business we hoped was finished."

She said, "I don't like the sound of this."

"And it's local."

"I have reason to like and dislike that."

He said, "Me, too. It has to do with ODESSA."

She groaned. "I was afraid of that. What's happening now?"

"Nothing specific, just some chatter they've picked up. It had been quiet for a while, and now it's not. That's what's got the agency's attention."

"I hoped I'd never heard the name ODESSA again."

He said, "You can knock down evil for a time, but it always seems to have a way of resurfacing."

"Very true. What do they want us to do, if anything?"

"It was a FYI type of call. I told them we could help if needed. Thought you'd be in agreement."

She grabbed a towel from the shower curtain bar and began to dry herself. "You knew if it involved ODESSA I'd say yes without asking. Does it involve a certain local somebody?"

"Yes. Maybe somebodies. It's hard to read the tea leaves at this time. You know they're not going to broadcast their intentions to the world."

"True. Not unless they're trying to mislead us."

He said, "ODESSA? Mislead us? No way."

They both laughed, and she pulled the curtain open. She had her towel wrapped around her. "Why, Mr. Smith. You have your boxers on. Didn't you get the memo? Towels were the proper attire."

"Sorry, must have been a communications breakdown. Let me get properly attired." He dropped his underwear to the floor, grabbed a fluffy white towel and wrapped it around his middle. "See? Better."

She nodded. "Much better. One more important question. What was his reaction to your question about the agency's direction?"

"He erased my question and went to a one-on-one secure line. He said I wasn't the only one wondering the same. It seemed like decisions by the top brass were being more so determined by politics than what was right."

"That's always been a problem."

He said, "But we both agreed it's been getting worse. I was glad I wasn't the only one to see this."

She said, "You don't think he's setting you up, do you?"

"No. Nothing worse than someone who stabs you in the back, especially a RED."

She nodded. "Yes. Retired Extremely Dangerous. That's us, REDs. Enough on that. There's still one problem."

"What's that?"

"You're now suitably attired, but you're still a dirty old man. Hit the showers. Then come see me, big boy."

He said, "Can it be a quick one?"

She grinned. "The shower, yes. The fun time, no." Her grin grew larger. "Reminds me of a story I heard about a pastor's wife. She'd been away at a women's retreat and gotten home just before the evening service started. She handed him a folded note as he walked to the pulpit. She told him how much she missed him and how she was going to make him happy ASAP when they got in the privacy of their bedroom."

"And?"

"When he reached the pulpit, he looked at the note. Fortunately, he had the presence of mind not to read it out loud, but he blushed and then preached his shortest sermon ever. Needless to say, they had a good time. Are you ready for a really good time?"

"Most certainly. It will be a quickie shower."

"That's the only quickie you'll get today."

"Yabba dabba do. This won't take long." He dropped his towel and got in the shower.

She went to the bedroom and laid down on the bed. Her lover was coming soon. She dropped her towel, powdered herself, and put his favorite perfume on. She thought about ODESSA. How she hated that name. They would deal with them as needed. Now, she just needed her man. She heard the water in the shower stop. It wouldn't be long now. She smiled. Nothing like being married to your lover. She was so glad she could trust him with her life. She'd had to several times before and may need to again in the coming days.

Chapter 31

On an island in the Caribbean

"Gentlemen, I hope you enjoyed a sampling of what I have on my island. Look, but don't indulge. These girls know how to lead someone astray."

Five men sat in comfortable chairs in the semi-lit room.

"Mr. Ebbstein, your presentation is most convincing." A scantily clad young woman sat on the speaker's lap. She smiled at him and ran her finger seductively under his chin. "Most convincing."

"Thank you, Mr. Silverman."

"I heartily agree," said a second man. A woman in lingerie sat on his lap. The other three men also had women similarly attired, toying with them. They nodded in agreement.

"Thank you, Mr. Merkel. They're worth everything I pay them, and more." He paused. "Girls, you must go now. Fun time is over here. We have important business to discuss. The last one out, please shut the door."

The women gracefully got off of the men, smiled, and seductively walked to the door and exited.

Ebbstein watched the other men's eyes follow the women. They sighed when the last left the room. He smiled. He knew what motivates men—sex, money, influence, and power. With women like this, he'd built an empire. Many a man had visited his mansion and fell for a Delilah, his Sirens, his temptresses. And some women. He spoke, "Who could resist my beauties? I'm sure I can depend on your continued support. Those women have put presidents, prime ministers, little petty tyrants, dictators, movie stars, and many, many important people under my influence. You know a few of the favors I've provided for this group."

A third man spoke, "You have a very persuasive way of making your point."

"Thank you, Mr. Schiller."

The fourth man ran his finger under his chin like the young girl had done moments before. "Very impressive display. I believe you can count on us as we are counting on you, Herr Ebbstein."

"Please, Mr. Kohl, refer to me as Mister Ebbstein, not Herr. Loose lips sink ships, you know."

"You are correct. I will not slip up like that again." He laughed. "Even though you have a Jewish name, you're not Jewish? How can that be?"

"My family is pure German. They built the Ebbstein Castle in a fiefdom that now is part of central Germany. In the sixteen hundreds, one of my ancestors allowed industrious Jews expelled from Spain to settle. Little could he foresee the trouble his short-sided good deed would cause in the future. They multiplied and prospered, eventually dominating the town and taking its name as their surname, though they chose to drop one of the b's in it. The Nazis took care of the problem, so here I am with a name many take as Jewish. Rarely do I correct them. Often, it's better to have people believe you are someone you're not."

"Is that why we are all using Jewish names?"

"That is correct, Mr. Silverman. If by serious misfortune word got out of this meeting, what would they say? Just that I'd entertained a small group of Jewish businessmen. Your identities and real reason for being here would be camouflaged in plain sight."

"I like the way you think, Mr. Ebbstein. I'm glad we invited you into our group. We needed a somewhat outside source to work with. Thank you for your clandestine support in the past." He stopped. "Gentlemen, I believe it's time to discuss our American problem."

Three heads nodded in agreement. Over the next one-half hour, they held a spirited and forceful discussion. After covering all the bases, they called for a vote. Two voted to find a way to eliminate the problem, and two voted to ignore the problem and find a way around it. All eyes turned to Ebbstein.

Silverman said, "Well, Mr. Ebbstein. It's in your hands. Which way do we go?"

He sat back in his chair and stroked his chin thoughtfully. He shifted in the chair. Both sides had valid points and plans for dealing with their problem, but which was best. After a long pause, he said, "Gentlemen. I would like to think some more about this difficulty. The ramifications of action or inaction could be huge and have long-lasting consequences. I'd like to sleep on it, if you agree to allow me."

The men looked at each other calmly. Silverman spoke. "I believe we are in agreement that you should do that. Will you take long?"

"I will let you know early tomorrow. In the meantime, enjoy yourselves while you are here. You know where your rooms are.

Indulge yourselves. Enjoy the many pleasures available to you. Now, I must get back to my duties."

"Thank you, Mr. Ebbstein, for hosting us," said Kohl.

"It's my privilege."

They made small talk as they left the room. Women dressed in lingerie appeared and took his guests away, just as he'd planned. Now, he had to see that the politician and his wife from Little Rock were happy. An odd pair in how they both liked women. He had personality and knew how to use it to get what he wanted. He could tell the wife could be difficult to deal with and seemed to have an air of entitlement. She knew what she wanted, and no one better damn well get in her way. The man could be talked to and manipulated, but she...she scared him a little. He would have to deal with her carefully and not get burned. He's seen her temper and did not wish to be on the receiving end.

And what to do about the man in Florida? His unconscious mind would work on it tonight while he slept. He always had an answer after a good night's sleep. Would he live or die? By tomorrow, Ebbstein knew he'd have an answer.

Chapter 32

"Ruff." A few seconds passed. "Ruff." This time, it was louder.

Roger rolled over in his bed. *Was that K9? Had to be something important.* He opened his bleary eyes and said, "I'm comin', K9. Give me a minute." Roger put on his pants, went to the trailer door, opened it, and saw K9 wagging her tail.

"Ruff." She looked at her empty bowl. "Ruff."

"Oh, no. Major tragedy. Empty dinner bowl. At least you didn't kick my door like Snoopy does to Charlie Brown." Barefooted Roger went outside and opened the garbage can containing the dog food. "K9, have you been havin' a party with all your friends? I don't remember it being this low, but you're in luck. Got enough for one more meal." He filled her bowl.

"Hey, buddy."

Roger turned and saw a man standing next to a box truck with La-Z-Boy painted on the side.

"I got a delivery for a Mr. Roger Pyles. Is that you?"

"It is. Bring it on down. Gate's dummy locked."

"Is your dog friendly? She came to the fence and growled at me."

"I'll take care of the dog. Bring your delivery on down." He turned to K9. "You behave yourself. This fella's got something I ordered. He's okay. No biting. No growlin'. He's not Bill Kenney."

She growled after he mentioned the town Chief of Police.

"Behave yourself. I want you on your best behavior, understand?"

She barked and wagged her tail.

"Good girl."

The drop off went without a hitch. The deliveryman named Jake carefully unboxed the chair and set it up on the porch where Roger pointed. K9 even allowed him to pet her before he left. He thanked Roger for his purchase and mentioned he was one of their best customers, this being his third chair.

Roger grimaced and said he hoped this one lasted longer than the first two. He liked the chairs, and he hoped his string of bad luck with them was over. Roger said the chairs were great, but recently, his chairs must think they were in a demolition derby. The deliveryman seemed puzzled, but Roger chose not to elaborate.

After he left, Roger decided to go to Winn Dixie, get some dog food, and then stop at the Black Cat Café for breakfast. The trip to the shopping plaza went quickly, he did his shopping, and then walked into the café. Lester's daughter, Ruth, sat at a booth, and she looked glum.

"Well, hello there, missy. I haven't seen you in a while. You okay?"

She took a sip of her coffee and gave a weak smile. "I'm fine, Roger."

"You mind if I order and then sit with you?"

"No, that would be fine," she said flatly.

Roger said nothing more, ordered, and sat across from her at the booth. "Your dad's been a super help gettin' me back on my feet after the fire. Good old dependable Lester."

"That he is."

"You seem a little down. Am I readin' you right? What's wrong? Shouldn't you be at work?"

She said, "I'm playing hooky. I called in sick. I needed a day off."

"When was your last day off?"

"About a month ago."

"No wonder you're tired. Those aren't eight-hour days you put it. More like ten or twelve at that medical office."

"Or more," she said. "I'm tired and burned out."

A waitress brought Roger's order. "Here you go. Hope I wasn't interrupting something important."

Roger said, "It's okay. Thank you."

She left and Roger took a sip of his Black Cat Premium Blend coffee. "Good stuff. Ahhh. Can I tell you a story?"

"An honest to God story?" she asked.

"Well, more or less. It will cheer you up."

"I could use some cheering up."

Roger took another sip of coffee and then cleared his throat. "I found I was out of dog food. Didn't want poor K9 to go hungry, so just before I came over here for some breakfast, I stopped at the Winn Dixie. The line at the checkout was long and, just to make conversation, I guess, the lady behind me asked if I had a dog. Guess the two bags in my cart must have given it away. I almost said something snarky, but bit my tongue."

She snickered. "You? Say something snarky? I can't image. What did you say?"

"I told her I was on the dog food diet again. It's the perfect diet. Just carry some kibbles in your pocket and munch on one or two when you get hungry. Why, I lost 15 pounds last time, but ended up in the hospital.

"She asked what happened. Did you get poisoned by the dog food? By now, everyone in the line that had grown was listenin. No, of course not. I told her I bent over to smell a bulldog's butt, and got hit by a bike goin' by. The guy behind her was laughin' so hard, I thought he was goin' into cardiac arrest."

She looked at him with suspicion in her eyes. "Roger, did this really happen?"

He was sheepish. No, but I thought you could use a good laugh."

She smiled. "Yeah, I need some cheering up. Thanks."

"Something overwhelming you?"

"Just the cares of life."

"Been there. I think everyone gets there from time to time."

She said, "It's just one thing after another. They keep coming. There's no letting up. I never get a break. The sick and dying just keep coming on and on and on."

"Yeah, it's burnout. I know it happens to cops and other people in high stress professions. Can I give the doctor some advice?"

"I need it, don't I?"

Roger said, "You do. This works and it's parent tested. When my son got cranky, my wife got him a snack and then laid him down for a nap. There's a story in the Bible about how the prophet Elijah won a great victory, but then got frightened out of his wits by the evil queen, who wanted to kill him. He ran and ran for his life until he could run no more. God told him to sleep, and when he awoke, He fed him.

"The good doctor Roger, me, prescribes some of your favorite food to fill you up, and some rest. I know you love your work, but gettin' burned out, and becomin' a cranky, crispy critter won't do anyone any good."

He moved a little closer, "Rest today. Take tomorrow off if you need to. Yeah, the world's sufferin', but people still get married and have families. It's called hope. In spite of all the misery in the world, I know people who still have faith, trust, confidence, and find love. We all need friends. Just work on your attitude and things will get better."

She was quiet for a moment. "You sound like my dad."

"He's my friend and has given me great advice. You won't find a wiser man. He may not have much of an education, but he's one of the smartest and most honorable of men I've ever met."

She nodded. "He is. I forgot that."

Roger smiled. "That's easy to do. He's your dad."

She smiled back. "Very true." The smile dropped from her face. "Roger, your food got cold while you were cheering me up."

"Don't worry about it. They can heat it up. Are you hungry now?"

"I am, and I think I'm going to take a long nap this afternoon. Would you order something for me?"

Roger went to the order counter, handed them the plate to reheat, and ordered Ruth a big omelet which he paid for. His order came back first, but he waited until her omelet came. They said little as they ate. They finished quickly.

"Roger, you knew exactly what I needed. Thank you."

"Been there, too. Just wish all of life's problems were as easy to solve."

"Ain't that the truth?"

She gave him a big hug as they were leaving, which he enjoyed to no end.

As he drove to his new trailer with the dog food, he felt good and wanted to enjoy just feeling good. He knew that difficulties could lie around the next corner. The world is like that, stumbling from crisis to crisis. It may not be long before he needed some encouragement himself. He was glad he could pay it forward today.

Chapter 33

The next day

Roger watched as Lester made his way through his gate by Canaveral Flats Boulevard. The old black man moved well for a man of his age. Roger was uncertain how old he was. He had to be in his late 60s, if not older.

"Wake up, K9. We've got company comin'."

She rose to her four feet, yawned, saw it was Lester, gave a little woof, and wagged her tail so much her whole body shook from side to side.

"That's right, K9, he's a friendly, and I hope he's got good news." Roger yelled, "Come on down, Lester. Your welcomin' committee is waitin'. Need something to drink?"

He yelled back, "I'm hurrying as fast as these ole legs can take me. Ice tea would be fine. Make it sweetened, but please don't tell Ruth it was sweetened. She's always fussin' at me about my sugar."

Roger went inside and got two sweetened teas from the refrigerator. When he came out, K9 was doing a happy dance about Lester's feet. "Looks like you've got a friend."

"I do, and I know she smells the donut I have with me. Here you go, girl. Don't eat it in one bite," but she paid him no mind and wolfed it down.

Roger said, "Where's your manners, K9? Makes me wonder if I've got a dog or a hog?"

Lester said, "About like raising teenagers."

Roger laughed, "I expect so. When I was that age, I could seriously chow down on some food. Mom would ask if I had a hollow leg." He handed a sweetened tea to the old black man. "Have a seat. Tell me you have some good news."

He did as instructed, took a big sip of the tea, and smiled. "Aww, ain't nothin' says the South like strong, sweet tea. Thank you." He swallowed some more. "Yeah, I have some good news. I stopped at the local trailer dealer and found you a 3/2 double-wide that will work fine. It'll take a week or so to get here. He sold his last one on the lot day before yesterday. I asked about setup, and he gave me a price from ground up I couldn't argue with. Only thing I'll need to do is have the utilities ready."

"Utilities? That shouldn't be too hard, I'd think."

"Yup, water line and meter are there. Cocoa Water Department didn't do anything after the old Flanagan place burned down. Didn't ever put a lock on the shutoff. It'll be simple to run a new sewer line to the existing septic tank. Florida Power and Light should connect the electric line from the existing pole to the weatherhead line on the new place. Should go smoothly, I hope."

Roger asked, "Weren't you goin' to get some help from some guys you knew?"

"I was, but one got in trouble. He's in jail. Another died and didn't bother to tell me, and a third is working full-time nights at Disney World. It was thanks, but no thanks. So that left me with one fella, and he'll do the ditch digging for the water and sewer lines."

Roger nodded. "Sounds like a plan. Looks like you'll getterdun with plenty of time for Gloria to move in."

"I believe so, but with construction, count on something going wrong. Seems like it always happens. Murphy's Law is real. If it's not done on time, it won't be for lack of trying or indecision." Lester smiled and laughed.

"What's so funny?"

"That brought back memories of my sister, Myrtle. God rest her soul. That girl could never make up her mind. Mom would ask Myrtle what she wanted in her sack lunch for school. She'd give her about three or four choices. Myrtle'd hem and haw and finally say, 'American cheese and plain bologna', after great deliberation. Exasperated, Mom would fuss, 'Myrtle, you have that every day. Don't you ever want something else? We have several kinds of each I got from the deli at Publix.' Truth was, she did want variety, but could never make up her mind."

Roger said, "So, bland cheese and bologna was her go to."

"That it was. It's a wonder she didn't go to school in her underwear. Thank God all she had were white panties. It took forever for her to decide on which blouse and skirt. Mom finally gave up and got her two changes, both the same."

"Now, that's funny."

"You think that's funny, once she asked some friends over, but had trouble deciding what night. She went back and forth between two nights, and forgot who she invited on which night. A few showed up the first night, and she had food to feed an army that night. The next night, the rest showed up and found her in curlers and a robe. All she had for food was leftovers, and her husband wasn't there. He was out with the boys playing cards and drinking a few."

Roger said, "You are serious? You're not makin' this up?"

"Oh, it gets better. After the last guest left, she decided to move the living room furniture around again. Her husband came in late and tipsy, forgot his wife's habit of moving things around because she could never decide which way was best, didn't turn on a light, tripped over a coffee table, fell, and broke his leg."

"Indecision. Sounds like Robert Frost's poem, *The Road Not Taken.*"

"If he'd been writing about my sister, she'd still be sitting at the fork in the road trying to figure which way to go. No road less traveled. No road most traveled. Just sitting there as life passed her by."

Roger asked, "Are you exaggeratin'? You have to be."

"Maybe a little, but not much." He stopped and took another sip. "Good tea."

"Thanks. It's bottled."

"Lipton label on the glass bottle kind of gave it away. Still good." He paused. "Thanks for talking with Ruth. She gets in a funk like that every now and then. Sometimes, it's hard to get her out of it."

"I've been there," Roger said. "I know the signs. Walk a mile in someone else's shoes can give you a lot of understanding and empathy."

"Very true."

Lester asked, "Got time to chase a rabbit down a hole?"

Roger smiled. "I can't think of anyone else I'd rather chase one with."

Lester let out a breath. "Okay, let me tell you some things I've learned in life, about this old world, and if you're game, about you."

"Sounds interestin'. The last parts not gonna be a Dutch uncle type of lecture, is it?"

"It will be firm, but benevolent."

Roger said, "Then proceed. Someone once told me wisdom starts by listening at the feet of an elderly person."

Lester grunted. "Elderly is always my present age plus ten years. Don't forget it."

"I feel wiser already."

"A wise man knows why God gave us two ears and one mouth."

"Point taken." Roger smiled and went silent.

Lester said. "Good. Now let me begin..."

Chapter 34

Lester started, "There's not too many people I trust in life, Roger, but I trust you. Trust is when you throw a baby in the air, and they laugh unafraid. They know you'll catch them. Pastor Nassey would say God's like that, I'm sure, if he were here. There are very few people and organizations made up of people you can trust.

"Some people say trust, but verify. That's good advice, but depending on who you're dealing with, don't trust. Verify. The news media is like that. They give out so much misinformation. For example, if you listened to them, you'd think the cops were at war with unarmed black men killing them all the time. How many cases of that actually happen in America yearly do you believe there are?"

Roger said, "Not sure. 1000? 10,000?"

"Try about 10 a year."

"Really?"

"Yes, really. Tell you something else I know. The more educated people are and trust what the news media says, the more ignorant they are. The more distorted their view of reality."

Roger thought for a moment. "You're right. That's been my experience when I was a college professor. You wouldn't believe how many of the people there I associated with thought they were so wise, but gave up thinkin' a long time ago. A hermit livin' in a shack in the woods was better off than a man havin' a graduate degree and bein' a cable news junkie."

Lester said, "If you want a blanket rule, trust no one. Verify everything. It will save you a lot of disappointment."

He shifted in his seat and took another swig of tea. "Some time ago, I mentioned Booker T. Washington, one of my heroes. He pulled himself up out of slavery. He gave us a warning over a century ago, quote, 'I am afraid that there is a certain class of race-problem solvers who don't want the patient to get well, because as long as the disease holds on, they have not only an easy means of making a living but also an easy medium through which to make themselves prominent before the public.' Unquote, and that hasn't changed.

"Even radical Malcolm X could see it. He knew there was slavery of the body, but today we have slavery of the mind, and today's slaves don't even realize they're slaves. Be careful what to allow in your head. People, the media, can make the innocent guilty, and the guilty innocent. It's all about control and power. They have the ability to influence minds, ideas, behaviors, and the attitudes of the masses, both black and white. The media can make you believe you are a victim, someone morally right always, not accountable nor responsible, and forever entitled to sympathy."

Roger said, "Lester, seems like you hit a hot spot."

His brows tightened. "No kidding. I'm just getting started. You got people being blamed for stuff that happened before they were born, and others not held responsible for what they do today. They teach you to hate yourself, boys to hate their sex, women to hate being feminine, and people to hate their country. You got people out there trying to change marriage, even eliminate it. Be careful. Don't ever take down a fence until you know why it needed to be put up. This country ain't perfect, far from it, but it sure beats whatever's in second place by a country mile.

"We all need to just be Americans. I hate Black History Month. You can't relegate my history to a month. And I hate the term, 'African-American.' It makes us all seem alike. No one uses the term European-American. They treat Africa like it's a country when it's a continent full of all kinds of people of all kinds of colors and differences. Hey, we're all mongrels just like white folk, just like the rest of the human race."

Lester said, "I usually don't talk about this, but I'm getting riled up, and this needs to be said. Seems like whenever the agitators get people acting and not thinking, black businesses and neighborhoods burn, and black people die. They don't want to work to fix things, only tear things down and rule the ruins. People that think analytically and independently won't follow them and their destructive ways. Real education's their enemy, so the schools keep turning out failures easy to control.

"You know, Roger, I think most white folk are ashamed and feel guilty about the history of slavery. It wasn't fair. I can see why people are angry, but I do know this. Since the Civil War, blacks have made tremendous gains. Black folk are great at sports, entertainment. They're inventors, military leaders, entrepreneurs, even some of the world's richest people. I think I'll live to see a black president, and I hope it's one that wants to build up America, not change it and tear it down."

Lester shifted in his seat uneasily and creases appeared in his weathered old black forehead. "But some things worry me. Some things are going backward. The government has transitioned charity into a legal entitlement to buy votes, and it's produced donors without compassion and recipients without gratitude to those who worked to provide it for them. We used to have married black folk making families. Tear a fence down, and you better be prepared for what's on the other side. May be angry dog, or worse. We need to be repairing fences that keep us safe, not removing them.

"We survived racism and Jim Crow, but now kids don't even know who their daddy is. While some things are better, some are worse, and they're both by design. God help us pick the right thing and do the right thing."

Neither man said anything for a few moments.

Finally, Lester spoke. "I usually don't talk like this. So many people I know can't handle the truth."

Roger shifted in his chair. "That was quite an impassioned speech. I consider myself lucky you trust me enough to tell me all that."

"I know why we get along. We're both contrarians. We do something most people won't do. We think. We use our heads for more than hat racks."

Roger laughed.

Lester smiled. "They say you can be honest with a true friend, and should only be completely honest with a true friend. Anyone else doesn't want to know the complete truth and can't handle it. People like that may and will use the truth against you."

"Sad to say, but I believe you're right. I've heard of people in the cities on the coasts so lonely they have to rent friends. You can hire them by the hour just to be with you, talk with you, or accompany you to an event. I've even heard of elderly people in Japan so desperate to have someone to talk to that they commit crimes to go to jail, so they can have the companionship of other inmates."

Lester said, "It's very sad. A true friend is there when you need him, and it takes time invested to have one."

Roger nodded. "Yeah. It does."

They sat in silence for a few moments.

Lester said, "That about wore me out. Think I'll go home and take a nap, but before I do, I'll make a few calls and make sure your new place is still moving forward."

"A nap sounds like a good idea."

K9 yawned.

Roger smiled. "Looks like even K9 agrees."

"So she do. Got to go. Till next time, Roger."

Lester's car soon disappeared down the road.

"Well, K9, that old black man never ceases to amaze me. No wonder he's gone as far in life as he has. We could use more people like him."

K9 gave a happy yelp and settled down on the floor. Her eyes soon closed, and she drifted off to sleep. It wasn't long before Roger was snoring in his new chair, too, taking some advice he'd recently given.

Chapter 35

Roger pulled his old truck up to the new house. He smiled as he thought of the promise it held. So many good things could happen here. There was so much potential.

"Not bad. I think I'm going to like it, Dad."

"I think everyone's gonna like it, Carlos. Your mom's got a bigger place without a rent increase and more privacy. No more noisy neighbors on the other side of a wall."

"Yeah, mom was always complaining about the couple next door. Getting drunk and hollering about this and that. They even threw plates at each other once. And, boy oh boy, was their making up noisy."

Roger rolled his eyes. "Yeah, I remember your mom mentioning it to me. Those walls must have been paper thin."

Carlos laughed. "Yeah, they got so loud, she couldn't stand it anymore, and we went to McDonald's. After a big meal, she even got us dessert, so we'd be there longer."

"She left that part out of the story when she told it to me."

"Where is she? Mom left right behind us."

Roger said, "Yeah, she did, but she caught a red light and maybe some more after that. She'll show up. How about we unload the truck in the meantime?"

"Sure thing, Dad."

They got out and carried boxes into the new house. They had Roger's pickup truck unloaded, heard a truck pull up outside, and saw Gloria in the driver's seat of a mid-sized U-Haul truck. Carlos said, "I don't think Mom's much of a truck driver."

Roger said, "I told her I'd drive it, but she insisted. She's a hardhead. Anything a guy can do, she thinks she can do as well."

"Mom's pretty tough... and stubborn."

"You hit the nail on the head, Carlos. She said she'd driven a manual transmission, but everything about that truck was manual, no power steering or brakes. I knew it would be a bear to drive, but she insisted, though I will say this. She did get it here. Let's find out what happened and get all the stuff in the house."

"Yeah, going to be fun. All the big stuff. Beds, tables, and furniture."

Roger said, "Yeah, gonna take all three of us to get some of that stuff in here."

"Yup."

They went outside. Gloria got out of the truck and slammed the door. She looked at Roger. "Don't say it. You were right."

"Say what? You made it."

She growled. "Manual transmission. Been a while since I drove one."

Roger said, "You wouldn't believe how many people don't know how to drive a manual."

"Oh yes I would. And manual everything else, and it all gave me challenges. And the traffic. Is there a launch today?"

"I think the Air Force is sending up something today, a big Atlas rocket, or maybe it's a Delta. I can't keep them separated."

"Traffic was terrible. You can't see very well in this big box truck. I'm not used to anything this big, and all you have are tiny mirrors to see behind you."

"What happened?" Roger asked.

"You know how you got to get in the left lane where Courtenay Parkway and Route 528 intersect?"

"Yeah."

"Well, nobody would let me over, so I had to continue up Courtenay till I could find a place to turn around. When I got to the Barge Canal, the bridge was going up, so I had to wait on it, and then it seemed like it didn't want to go down. It took forever. I heard people at work complaining about the bridge and now I've seen it firsthand, I agree. It's a royal pain."

Roger said, "Yeah, I saw an article in the paper about that. Said they're gonna overhaul both sides, north and southbound, one side at a time. Could take several months and that's weather permitting."

Gloria shook her head. "Enough about the trip here and bridge problems. Let's get this stuff in. Weatherman said it could rain today, and it's getting cloudy."

"Okay, Mom. Let's go," Carlos said.

Roger smiled and nodded.

They spent the next three hours unloading the truck and carrying heavy and bulky items into the new home. Gloria directed where she wanted the furniture for now. Once settled in, she could move things around if needed. Roger saw Carlos roll his eyes behind his mother, but managed to keep a straight face.

They made another trip to Gloria's apartment. Gloria drove the U-Haul there, but told Roger he could drive back when the truck was loaded up. Somehow, he bit his tongue and never said, "I told you so." He thought it, and it showed on his face, though he tried not to. She said nothing, just smiled.

They loaded the trucks full. Everything left would fit in her car for the last run tomorrow. They got some burgers at McDonald's. Everyone was hungry and ate heartily. After returning to the new place, the three people unloaded the truck, but it didn't go as fast as the first time. They plopped down in the living room chairs.

Roger said, "I don't know about you, but I'm beat."

Gloria said, "I second that."

Carlos nodded. "Me, too."

Gloria said, "Thank you, Roger, for your help."

"What about me?" Carlos blurted out.

She gave a weary smile. "You, too, son. I didn't forget you." She sighed. "I'm bushed." Her eyes went to Roger. "If you don't mind, I think I'm going to clean up and head to bed. And you too, Carlos."

"Aw, Mom. I wanted to talk to Dad."

Roger said, "Your Mom's right. I'm tired, too. You have a school day tomorrow."

"Oh, alright, if I must." He walked to his room, dragging his feet as he went.

Gloria said, "I think he's going to like having you close."

Roger said, "Yeah, me too, but we need our rest. Wish I had his energy."

"Me too. I'll take him to school tomorrow, and you meet me at the apartment. We'll get the last load and return here."

"I think you might have more than can fit in your car."

She nodded. "After thinking about it, I do, too. We'll make it work."

"Yeah." Roger got up and Gloria did too.

She went to Roger and gave him a hug. "Thank you, Roger, for all you've done. I don't know how this is going to work out between us, but it's off to a good start. At least, we're not at each other's throats by now."

Roger hugged her back and drew away. "I better be goin'."

"Yeah, I guess so. See you tomorrow. Bye."

"Bye."

Roger walked to his truck and got in, but it wouldn't start. "Damn." He got out and kicked a tire. "Stupid truck."

He walked to his new trailer across the street. K9 greeted him with a happy dance. He went inside, relieved himself, and washed his face and arms to the elbows. K9 welcomed him again back to the porch. He sat down heavily in the La-Z-Boy chair. He scratched her head and said, "Been a long, tiring day, girl, and now my stupid truck won't start. What else can go wrong?"

Weary Roger and K9 slowly drifted off to sleep.

Tomorrow would be another day with its challenges.

Chapter 36

The Next Morning

Roger woke much refreshed. He took a quick shower and dressed. A hungry K9 greeted him at the door. "K9, as a girl, could you tell me something that's puzzlin' me? You get hungry and you're happy to see me. Women get hungry and it turns to hangry, you know, hungry flavored with anger. Wish they could be more like you."

He opened the trash can containing the dog food. K9 crowded about his legs, nearly knocking him over. "Easy girl. I'm not gonna be much good to anyone with a broken leg or two. Easy, K9, take it easy."

The hungry dog paid him no mind. Only after he filled her bowl did she leave him alone.

"Eat quick, K9. I see the cat waitin' for you to finish. I'm surprised Donkey and the little horse aren't here. They could pull the Welcome Wagon." Movement near the barn caught his eye. "There they are. Looks like the equines had a good night. Now, pardon me, girl, while I have my breakfast." She continued to eat and ignore him. Roger grunted. "Thanks. You're welcome, too."

He put a breakfast bowl in the microwave and fired up Mr. Coffee. The brew finished first, and Roger sat contented sipping as the bell on the microwave sounded. A banana finished off his meal.

Done, he walked across the road and tried to start the truck, but it was still dead. He looked under the hood and saw the battery terminals were corroded. He found a rusty crescent wrench under the seat, tapped the terminal connection sharply, tried the ignition switch, and the truck started. He smiled and muttered, "It was somethin' simple. Maybe my luck's changed." He'd clean and fix the connection later. Gloria would be expecting him.

His trip to Gloria's place on Merritt Island was uneventful. Traffic flowed freely until he got to Courtenay Parkway. It seemed like he caught every red light. Life happens.

Gloria answered on the second knock. "There he is, Mr. Sleep till noon. Glad you could make it."

"Remember, I had to get my truck runnin'." Roger fibbed. "It wasn't an easy fix. Electrical problem. I had a devil of a time figurin' out what the issue was."

"Glad you could fix it. Let's get to work. I have more things to box up. I'll do that, and you carry them out."

"Oh, I see. Get the big, strong man to do all the heavy liftin'."

She said, "Sounds good to me," and went into the bedroom.

Roger threw up his hands and started carrying the bulky boxes down the stairs. He was glad it was all downhill. Every time he carried one down, another full one took its place. He grumbled, "Hope she runs out of boxes soon."

Slowly, the pile got smaller until it was no more. His truck was full. The only empty spot was the space for the driver. He filled her trunk and put some clothing in the back seat space. When he walked up the steps, he was half-expecting to see more boxes, but there was no more. Gloria sat on an upside-down five-gallon bucket.

"Man, didn't know I had so much stuff," Gloria said.

"You gave me a workout. Don't think I have to go to the gym tonight."

"Roger, I didn't know you were a gym rat."

"Guess I'm busted. I ain't been in a gym since college, and that was just to impress the ladies with my muscles."

"You're full of it."

Roger grinned. "Busted again. Now, are you gonna insult your free help, or are we gonna get this stuff to your new place before I change my mind about volunteerin'?"

"Point taken. Let's go."

About 20 minutes later, they arrived at Gloria's new abode. They emptied the truck, got her dresses out of the car, and took a break. She took a chair, and Roger sat on her couch.

"Thank you, Roger, for being so helpful. This new place should work out well. Carlos said he likes the idea of you around. I like that, too. Maybe we could, you know, actually become a family."

"Yeah, you never know. Seems like we got the conjugal part down pat."

She smiled and looked off thoughtfully. "Yeah, guess we do. You make a good lover."

Roger grinned. "Never had any complaints."

She hit his upper arm.

"Ow. What was that for?"

She said seductively, "Because you're a big, irresistible hunk, that's why."

"Guess I am. What are you gonna do about it?"

"This."

Gloria got up and sat in his lap. She put her arms around him. He did the same.

Roger said, "You know, I'm beginning to get ideas."

"I hoped so."

"You sure we should be doin' this?"

Gloria said, "No, but it was so much fun the last time."

"It was, even with the little interruption."

"Well, the little interruption, our son, is in school, and I don't have to pick him up until schools out. We have at least three hours to ourselves."

"I see." He kissed her and lusty passions overcame both of them. After some steamy time on the couch, they got up and Roger carried her into the bedroom. He closed the door, though they were the only ones there.

***

Two Hours later

"Nuts!"

Roger woke with a start. "What's wrong, Gloria?"

"We fell asleep. I got to get Carlos. Nuts!"

They dressed in a hurry, and Gloria sped off in her car down Canaveral Flat's Boulevard. Roger watched it disappear. "Here we go again." He got in his vehicle and turned the ignition key. Nothing happened. He tried it again. More nothing. He grabbed the crescent wrench and tapped the battery terminals. Once more, he tried the ignition switch. Nothing. One more attempt gave the same results. "Here we go again. Maybe my luck hasn't changed at all."

He sighed and walked across the street to his new place. K9 was hungry, so he fed her. Seeing her eating heartily reminded him he was hungry, too. He placed a TV dinner, broccoli with beef, in his microwave oven, and it was ready in three minutes.

He grabbed a beer from the refrigerator and sat down to eat. The meal needed salt, and pepper, and Mrs. Dash, and soy sauce, and a tad of Louisiana Hot Sauce. He grumbled to himself. "Don't think I'll ever buy that brand again. Cardboard would taste better." He ate half and gave the rest to K9, who sniffed it and walked away. "That settles it. When a dog won't eat it, it's now officially on the never-buy-again list."

He kicked back in his La-Z-Boy chair, picked up a Louis L'Amour novel about the old West, and began to read. About 45 minutes later, he saw Gloria pull up to the doublewide. Five minutes later, she walked down the lane to his new trailer with Carlos beside her. She had a frustrated look on her face.

When she got close, Roger asked, "Why the sour look? Is there a problem?"

"Yeah, Mr. Landlord. There's a problem. Actually two. No water and no electric. Got any idea what's going on?"

"No, I'm clueless, but let me slip my shoes on, and I'll be right over and take a look."

As he put on the shoes, she asked, "Why's your truck still across the street? Did you need some more exercise?" She grinned.

"No, got plenty of exercise today with all the physical activity. The truck didn't want to start again. I messed with the battery, but it still wouldn't start. May have to give my favorite shade tree mechanic a call."

They made small talk as they walked. He checked the water first. As she said, nothing was coming out of the faucets anywhere in the place. And the shutoff in the line between the trailer and the ground was on. He went to the water meter box and opened the lid. "Uh-oh. I found the problem. There's a lock on the shutoff. I bet the water company did it. Guess I'll have to give them a call on Monday. They're closed for the weekend."

Gloria said, "I so wanted this to go smoothly, but I should have known better."

"Yeah, that makes two of us. Let me check the electric. Maybe it's just a tripped breaker." Roger said.

The trio went around the building to the master panel. Roger opened it and groaned. "This ain't lookin' good."

"How bad is it, Dad?"

"The master breaker's fried and maybe a few smaller breakers below it. This ain't lookin' good at all. The trailer dealership's closed for today. Someone should be there working for the weekend, but we're out of luck until then."

Carlos said, "So, what are we going to do?"

Roger glanced at Gloria. Her face told him she had the same question. "Well, several options. You could stay here and live with it until it's fixed."

"No," Gloria said. "Next option."

"Hotel?"

"No, I'd rather not."

Carlos said, "We could move in with Dad until the problem's solved."

Roger hesitated before he spoke. He looked at Gloria for a reaction, but she gave none. "You are correct, Carlos. You guys could stay with me till it's completely livable."

Roger looked at her with a "Well?" expression on his face.

Gloria seemed to be considering the options. She sighed. "Guess it's the last option. Don't seem to be any others."

Carlos smiled. "Alright!"

"Guess you guys stay with me for a couple of days. Carlos, you get the small bedroom. Gloria, you can have mine, and I'll sleep on the big couch."

Gloria said, "I don't want to take your bed, Roger. I'll sleep on the couch."

"No you won't. You're my guests and I insist. I'm not takin' no for an answer."

"Well Carlos, looks like your father has spoken, and I don't think we can talk him out of it. I've heard about how stubborn people that grew up in the Appalachians can be."

"Stubborn as a Cuban?" Carlos said.

Roger said, "Slightly worse."

"Wow. That's stubborn."

All three laughed.

Gloria looked around. "Guess we need to grab a change of clothes and get the food out of the refrigerator."

Roger said, "Let's get to it. You guys had supper? I did while you were gone."

"No, but I have some things inside that need eaten. Let's go. Let's get this done. I'm hungry."

"Me too," said Carlos.

They put their clothing in a small suitcase and placed the food in some empty cardboard boxes left over from moving. The food, especially the frozen food that included a turkey, was heavy. Roger grunted as he carried it to her car. Carlos took their full suitcases. They were heavy, but somehow, he managed. Gloria then drove them across the road to Roger's trailer.

"What about your truck?" Gloria said.

"It's not goin' nowhere. See if I can get it runnin' tomorrow morning. If not, I'll call a mechanic for help."

They filled up Roger's refrigerator, and Gloria heated up some leftovers. They ate, cleaned up the table, sat down, and had a long chat about anything and nothing. No one seemed bored. Daylight turned to darkness, and their eyes got heavy. Roger made sure everyone was comfortable in their beds and went to the coach. He placed his outerwear on a nearby chair. Wearing only his tighty-whities, he laid down on the coach and pulled a sheet over him.

He stared at the ceiling. Life sure has its challenges. Guess you gotta roll with the punches and make the best of it. He could already hear Gloria snoring. She sounded like she was getting a head cold. Not a fun thing to have. Today had been busy, tiring, stressful, and a little fun. He hoped tomorrow would be better.

Roger said a short, quick prayer and drifted off to sleep.

Chapter 37

KABOOM!!

Roger rolled off the coach onto the floor. His heart felt like it would pound out of his chest. "What the..."

Yellow-orange light poured into the trailer. He looked at the watch on his arm. 4:30. What's going on? He saw a figure in the hallway.

"Roger? Are you okay?"

"I'm on the floor, but I'm okay. What's goin' on? Where's Carlos?"

"He's behind me. I think the new place blew up, and it's on fire."

Roger got to his feet, swearing as he rose. "I don't believe it." Carefully, he peaked out a window. It was true. He swore again.

She said, "Do you have a gun?"

"No, it burned up in the fire here."

"I have one."

His eyes adjusted between the light and dark. Gloria stood a few feet away. She wore a knee-length T-shirt that clung to her breasts, that rose and fell with her rapid breathing. He saw the gun in her hand, her finger in the ready position. A frightened Carlos stood behind her. "Good. Wish I had a phone to call for help."

Gloria said, "What about your cell phone?"

"It's dead. Forgot to charge it."

"What about the phone I saw on the kitchen wall?"

"Lester must have had it installed. I hadn't called the phone company to get a new landline." Crouching down, he made his way to the kitchen and found the phone. "It's got a dial tone. I'll call 9 1 1."

The operator answered on the third ring. Roger explained his problem. She said she would alert the police and fire units. Stay put. Stay safe. Roger said he would.

Roger took a quick look out the window. The fire across the street still burned brightly and intensely.

Carlos said, "What do we do, Dad? I'm scared."

"We wait for backup. Your mom's got a gun. We'll be safe. We stay here until the cavalry arrives."

It seemed like an eternity before someone arrived. He could hear someone outside. Gloria tensed, ready for action.

"Roger, are you okay?" It was Bill.

"I am. Gloria and Carlos are with me. Is it safe to come outside?"

"Stay where you are. We need to wait for more help."

Bill had no more said that than they heard a siren sound followed by many more, and they were coming their way. Fire trucks and police vehicle descended on the area. They were soon thick as ants on a piece of candy. Blue and red lights added to the light of the fire.

Roger said, "We need to get some clothes on. I think our day has started early."

Gloria nodded. "Time to get dressed, son."

"Yes, Mom."

They went to their rooms. Roger quickly dressed. Carlos was first out, followed by Gloria, dressed in her police uniform with her tactical belt. She was ready for whatever was waiting.

"Bill, can we come out now?" Roger said.

"I think so. Be alert. I think the situation is under control, but you never know."

"We're comin' out."

Roger opened the door and looked around. Bill was in his uniform, and he had his gun ready. The fire burned furiously. It almost seemed alive. Flames shot skyward, brightening the night sky. He swore. "Unbelievable."

Gloria followed him, gun in hand. Her eyes read of tenacity, fear, and pain. She swore, too, when she saw the inferno.

Bill said, "You guys stay here. I'll get the police and fire commanders. I know they want to speak with you."

They both nodded. Gloria stood ready with her gun. A few minutes later, Bill returned with two men full of questions. Do you live here or at the house on fire? Is there anyone else in there? What happened? Do you know what started the fire? Are you okay?

Roger and Gloria answered them directly, but no, they did not know what caused the fire. They were asleep here. A loud boom, possibly an explosion, woke them up. Satisfied with the answers, all three went across the street to the fire that was now under control. Even so, Roger and Gloria both knew the double-wide home was a total loss.

Carlos ran down the steps to his mother and threw his arms around her. "Mom!" He began to cry, and she did, too. Roger went to them and hugged them both. His eyes were moist. He said, "We'll get through this. Somehow, we will. Where there's life, there's hope."

Several minutes passed, and Bill and another cop returned to Roger's trailer.

"Roger," Bill said, "You're the homeowner, so I need to speak with you, alone. Deputy Swanson will stay here with Gloria and Carlos." She looked at him suspiciously, but said nothing. Her eyes clearly stated she knew what was going on.

Roger and Bill walked to the road. Donkey and the little horse watched the fire from the shed.

Bill said, "I think you know why we're here."

"Yeah, the fire wasn't an accident. Someone set it."

"Yeah, it was arson."

Roger said, "It wasn't me."

"I know it wasn't. This was done by professionals, but they missed, fortunately. Why wasn't Gloria and the kid in the new place?"

"Someone put a lock on the water meter shutoff, and the main electric breaker shorted out. It was scorched black. The place had no utility service. They were stayin' with me until we could get it all fixed and sorted out."

Bill said, "You better thank your guardian angels for watching over you."

"I will."

"Any idea who'd want you dead? They probably saw your truck and thought you were inside."

Roger said, "I'd put my money on ODESSA."

Bill nodded. "That would be my first thought. Everything's under control now. The firemen will get the fire out, and you already gave the police a statement. It would be in your best interest to be tight-lipped about what happened tonight. I can guarantee this isn't the end of this story. I think some heavy hitters are going to show up."

"I do, too."

They made small talk to lighten the mood. The firemen had the fire out in the next hour. They left a truck with a skeleton crew to deal with any flare-ups. One deputy stayed with them and another sat in front of Roger's trailer. Roger knew this wasn't over by a country mile.

Gloria had the coffee on, and a cup was waiting for him when he got back to the trailer.

"I made coffee for you."

"Thanks."

She said, "You hungry?"

"No. You?"

"No. For some reason, my appetite has left me."

He smiled. "I can't imagine why."

"What now, Roger? You know who did this and why."

"Yeah. I believe I do."

"What are we going to do? I'm scared?"

Roger said, "I am, too, but I know we have some hidden friends in high places, or we wouldn't be here today."

"That's good to know. Care to tell me more?"

"Not at this time. Maybe later. Trust me."

She was silent for a moment. "Okay. Guess I'll have to trust you."

"I'd tell you more if I could."

She rose and gave him a kiss on the cheek. "Think I'll try to get some sleep. Carlos is already down."

"Okay, not sure I can."

She nodded and disappeared down the hallway.

Roger sighed deeply. *Now what?*

He shook his head. He wished he knew.

Chapter 38

At the back side of Canaveral Flats

"Well, Mr. Smith, you pulled it off again. Roger Pyles and his family are safe. Tell me how you did it. I'm all ears. Give me the details I don't know."

"I will, but I couldn't have done it without you watching my back. You never know when things can go south, and you have to go to Plan B."

"But it all went well, right?"

"Yes, my wife, AKA Mrs. Smith. It went very well. Roger had vehicle troubles at just the right times, and for plausible and simple reasons that I created."

"What about the problems at the double-wide?"

"A simple lock like the water company uses worked to shut off the water. When they contact the water company to get it turned on, the utility will realize they don't have a key. They'll think the lock was installed when the house burned years ago, and the paperwork and key have been lost. I purposely gave the lock an aging treatment. It looked old. They'll use a bolt cutter to remove the lock, and that will be that. Now, the electric. That was more complicated."

"So, what did you do?"

Mr. Smith said, "The agency gave me some of their James Bond type stuff when I told them what I wanted to do. It worked fine, a little too fine. Glad I did extra to prepare myself in case the arc flash was bigger than they told me it would be."

"I see. Never trust an electrician with singed eyebrows. Do you think the agency planned for a bigger flash that could have harmed you?"

"That thought crossed my mind. I don't know. Operations like this do have an element of risk. Do the best planning you can, and still things can go sideways." He stopped and touched his lips thrice. "I wonder..."

"I do, too," Mrs. Smith said. "I do, too. But you saved the bottle of wine that got them so drunk. It seems potent on Roger and Gloria."

"That's what we're drinking now. It's got a hell of a lot of alcohol in it."

Mrs. Smith said. "I thought so, too."

"Made it a whole lot safer and easier to disable Roger's truck after they were amorous and fell asleep."

She laughed. "Yes, I can see how this would loosen your inhibitions. It's sure got a kick." Her face turned serious. "Roger's a smart guy. Do you think he'll put two and two together and figure out what happened? He might even figure out who we are."

"He could. I wouldn't put it past him."

"What would we do then?"

He said, "We'll deal with it, if and when it happens. What we do know for certain is this operation exposed ODESSA's hand. The agency's learned some invaluable information about their network. I don't think they realize how much damage was done. And I got a personal thanks from the higher ups."

"That's good." She stood up. "Wow, this stuff is potent."

"I do believe you're not holding your alcohol very well. Are your inhibitions in a lowered state?"

She gave him a silly grin. "Why don't you find out?"

He turned the lights off. "Why, Mrs. Smith, they sure are."

Even in the half light, he could see the heat in her eyes. She slurred her speech. "Mizzer Smiff, you ain't seen noffin' yet. I may not hold my alkeyhall very well, but I can certnly hold on to you."

And even he was surprised at the fire the alcohol'd lit. It was a long time before they could contain it, and even longer for the fire to finally burn itself out.

Chapter 39

Ebbstein's Island

"Sorry I'm late," he said as he entered the room. "There was, shall I say, a situation that needed my personal attention." Four sets of eyes followed him. He took a seat.

"Mr. Ebbstein, we'd been told you would be late. We waited a short while and then began the meeting without you. I hope you were able to resolve the problem."

"It's been dealt with. What did I miss?"

"It was a short meeting. We're done. We took a vote on how to deal with the problem in Florida."

"Roger Pyles?"

"Yes," the other man said.

"And what was the outcome?"

"After a brief discussion about how we should go ahead, we made a decision. It was unanimous."

"Looks like my vote wouldn't have mattered," Ebbstein said. "What was your decision?"

"Roger Pyles has escaped all our numerous attempts to eliminate him. It's frustrating, but true. All frontal attacks have failed. We've wasted precious resources and have nothing to show for it. We decided to cut our losses, before those opposing us, learn more about us and cause damage we cannot afford. Unfortunately, some lower-level operations were exposed, and had to be sacrificed for the good of the greater cause. Our foes will be happy, and we will be able to continue. Operations will be regrouped, progress will slow down, even halt for a time, but the cause will remain intact and continue."

Ebbstein said, "But what about Pyles himself?"

The other man said, "There is a tactic in war. When the enemy has a stronghold you can't overcome, you isolate it and go around. You can come back later at a more convenient time and deal with it. That is what we decided to do."

Ebbstein nodded his head. "I see."

The men were silent for a moment.

The man who had been speaking for the group said, "If there are no objections, this meeting is adjourned, and we can attend to other business."

There were none.

Ebbstein said, "Will you be staying and enjoying yourselves further here on the island?"

"No, we must be on our way. There've been other setbacks for our organization besides dealing with Mr. Pyles. We must be off and see to them."

"That's a shame. The girls were expecting you, but I understand. Business before pleasure. Do you need anything more before you leave?"

"It's been taken care of, Mr. Ebbstein. We thank you for your hospitality."

The three other men nodded in agreement.

The meeting adjourned, and the men went their separate ways, leaving Ebbstein alone. He found a comfortable chair, but his thoughts were not comforting. What more had been discussed in his absence? What was his standing with the others now? He smiled to himself. A smile and his charm had gotten him out of difficult situations before. It should this time, too, but he wasn't sure. It only took one misstep to bring his empire down. He'd better enjoy it while it lasted.

Chapter 40

Roger's porch

Roger had nearly nodded off to sleep when he heard K9 bark. A car stopped on the shoulder in front of his place. *Pastor Nassey.*

The pastor opened the dummy-locked gate and walked toward Roger's new trailer. K9 ran to meet him, and was rewarded with lots of attention as she danced about his feet.

"Easy girl. You'll knock me over. Easy."

Roger yelled, "K9, have some manners. We don't kill our guests. Behave yourself." He heard the pastor laugh.

"Wish everyone was as happy to see me," Pastor said in a loud voice. "You got time to talk, Roger?"

"Sure, I always have time for you. Come on down." Roger went in the trailer and returned with two iced teas just as the pastor entered the screened-in porch. "Here you go, Pastor."

"Thank you. I needed one of those."

"You're welcome. Have a seat. What's on your mind?"

The pastor said, "Several things. You've been through a lot lately. Sick, a windstorm that damaged your old trailer beyond repair, a fire, and then another fire that destroyed your new double-wide. Plus, being sick again. You've had a lot to deal with. How are you holding up?"

Roger said, "Yeah, I have. I think I know how Samsonite luggage feels after being manhandled by a gorilla. I may not have any visible dents or scratches, but I sure feel beat up."

"I thought you might."

"You gonna give me a little sermonette?"

"Well, now that you asked for one, I will. Besides, you look like you could use some encouragement."

"Yeah, I could, but it gets even better?"

Pastor asked, How's that?"

"I didn't even have to go to church to get a sermon. It came to me."

"Guess it did."

"And no plate passed around."

The pastor laughed. "Don't bet on getting off that easy." He stopped. "And there is one big disadvantage for you."

"What's that?"

"You can't escape out the back door and go home. You are home. You can't run away."

Roger said, "I can't argue with that. Let's hear those good words."

The pastor cleared his throat. "You know me. I have to tell you what I believe, what makes life worth living."

"I think I know—Jesus, God, love, hope, and all that good stuff."

"You got it. It's not that I don't get down sometimes. When you look at the troubles and corruption in this world, it's easy to get depressed, but I believe, like David wrote in the Psalms, God's love is unending and without measure. If I go into the heavens, He's there. Our astronauts even took communion when they were on the moon, but God's love goes to the end of His creation, wherever that is. If I go into the depths of the ocean, I can't escape His presence. If I go into the deepest mine on the earth, He's still there. His love is unfathomable and unending. That gives me comfort to know He's always there for me. I'll never be alone."

Roger said, "I know what you're sayin'. You become what you think about. You know the story about the old Indian grandfather and his grandson. The boy told of the conflict he felt inside. Two wolves seem to be fighting for control. What should he do? The grandfather was quiet for a moment until he was sure he had his grandson's total attention and then gave him these words of wisdom. 'Only feed the wolf you want to make strong.'"

"Very true. This happened to me. I planted a garden and got busy for about a month. I told my seven-year-old daughter to water it. She did. Everything. I found her watering a weed, too. One grew huge and was crowding out the tomatoes. I asked her why she was watering the weed. She gave me an impish grin and told me she wanted to see how big it would grow. The weed grew so big it pushed out the tomatoes. I used it as a lesson for her on how bad things can push out good things. She liked tomatoes and told me to pull the weed up. I told her to pull it up. It was her weed. She tried and couldn't and asked for my help. It took both of us to uproot the weed. She got a lesson she'll never forget."

Pastor took a sip of tea. "We had a good laugh about it afterward. I think God wants us to laugh as much as we can. Being serious all the time can wear you down. I know God has a sense of humor. Look at some of the creatures He made. The duck-billed platypuses looks like it was made out of parts He had left over. And why did He make the giraffe with such a long neck and no voice, mammals that live in the sea, or birds with long legs that can't fly?

"God likes laughter. When His angels told Sarah she'd have a baby at ninety, she laughed."

Roger said. "I'm sure she did. Her eyes must have about rolled out of her head when she heard that. Nurse a baby at that age? Whoever heard of anything that crazy or impossible?"

"Did you know Abraham named their son Isaac? It means laughter."

"I knew Isaac was their son, but I didn't know the name's meaning."

Pastor said. "And God can work with anyone. Isaac's family life would be best described as dysfunctional, as was his son, Jacob's family life, but God worked with both of them, faults and all. I think He does that to show there's hope for everyone.

"Roger, the problem in this world is broken people, not more laws, or broken laws. The problem's in the hearts of men."

"I believe you're right, Pastor. There's evil and good in this world, hope and despair. People need something to believe in. I've found you can't depend on murder cases to give your life purpose. There's more out there."

"Keep looking, Roger. You'll find it."

"Yes, I believe I will. I think everyone can if they just think and look."

Pastor nodded. "Keep looking."

They sat in silence as they both milled over their own thought. After a while, Pastor spoke. "What about Peggy Sue?"

"What?"

"**You know what.** Peggy Sue's back. Mrs. Tallman's renegade daughter, AKA Cowboy Gene. What are you going to do?"

Roger stalled. "What are you gonna do?"

"Nothing. I'm a pastor and what I know's covered by clerical privilege. You don't have that. As a cop, you're supposed to turn her in."

"I know what the law says. The law can be a real ass when you follow the letter."

Pastor said. "No argument there. I know you'll make the right decision."

"Guess I'm gonna have to. I know you can't depend on murder. Guess I'll have to depend on myself, too."

"Very true, Roger. And God. He'll never let you down."

"Guess so."

Pastor said, "And with that thought and dilemma, I have to leave you. I have faith you'll reach the right conclusions. Thanks for the tea. Got to go. See you again."

"Thanks Pastor. See you, too."

The pastor's car soon disappeared down Canaveral Flats Boulevard. "K9, come here." She came through the hole in the trailer skirting, yawned, and went to Roger. "Good girl. That Pastor's a good man. He tells me things I need to hear, hard things. I can depend on him to tell me the truth, and you girl, to be there when I need you, and be a good listener. Now, it looks like it's up to me. Pastor says I'll make the right decisions. I trust he's right." He sighed. "I sure hope so."

And from K9's look, she seemed to think so, too.

Chapter 41

The Next Day

"Grrr."

"What is it, K9? What do you hear, girl?"

"Grrr."

A pickup truck stopped in front of Roger's old trailer.

"Grrr."

"Now, I see what got your attention. Not again. Our favorite flatfoot, Canaveral Flats' entire paid police force, Bill Kenney. He's sure makin' a nuisance of himself. You behave yourself and no biting. He'll leave a bad taste in your mouth. Maybe even give you rabies."

"Grrr."

"That's right. You've been vaccinated, but I don't think he has." Roger stroked the brown hair on the dog's head, and tickled under her chin. "No, I won't bite him, either, even if he needs it. I haven't been vaccinated against what he has. No point risking a life-threatening infection. You go under the trailer and stay out of trouble. I'll take care of the riff-raff."

She growled again and went through the opening in the trailer skirting.

"Girl, this could be interestin'. He's carryin' a Publix's paper grocery bag. That's unusual."

Bill opened and closed the gate carefully to not let the donkey escape. The donkey, which Roger just called Donkey, was especially curious about the bag, peeked inside, but soon lost interest, and drifted away, grazing as he went.

"Hey, Roger. You busy?"

Roger mumbled under his breath. "He's got me curious, K9."

"What did you say, Roger? I can't hear you."

He grunted. "No, I ain't very busy. Come on down."

Bill smiled and walked to Roger's dwelling. He opened the door to the screened-in porch and took a seat. "How's it going today?"

"Pretty good so far, but then you arrived. What's in the bag? Aren't you gonna raid my refrigerator for a beer or three?"

"No, not today. This is just a social visit to my old friend."

"Who would that be, me or K9?"

"Where is she? I didn't see her?"

"Grrr."

"Under the trailer behaving. Don't give her a reason to come out."

Bill smiled. "Two things. I think I found a home for your temporary house guest, Donkey."

"I decided to keep him."

"Yeah, I know. I was letting you know I knew. I could tell you were growing fond of him. You two are so much alike."

"Be glad I like you, or I would have run you off by now."

Bill said, "No, seriously, you're so much alike. For instance, he's a good judge of character, loyal, and trustworthy. A defender of others. If not for Donkey, that coyote would have killed K9."

Roger said, "That's true. He does have a lot of good points."

"But the two of you can be very stubborn, you only a little less."

"Now, you're tryin' my patience, Bill, what little I have." He paused. "What's in the bag? You got me curious."

"I come bearing gifts." He reached into the bag and pulled out a six-pack of Genesee Cream Ale beer. "Ever had one of these? Got another one, too."

"Are you kiddin'? We used to drive across state lines to get that stuff. Where did you get that? It's not distributed around here, not within a thousand miles."

"Took it off a bunch of underage college boys passing through. Gave them a choice, the easy way or the hard way. Surrender the beer and go on their way or argue about it and go to jail. They took the easy way."

"Smart boys. You can always get more beer, even if it's not Genny Cream Ale."

"I've heard it's good, but never had one."

Roger said, "Well, what are you waitin' for? Let's indulge."

Bill handed one to Roger and took one for himself. Two psssffffs sounded as they popped the tops and took swigs.

Roger said, "That was better than I remembered. What do you think?"

216

"Those college kids had good taste."

"You on duty?"

"No, my day off. Thought I'd mellow out and just chill."

"Excellent beer. So, the gift you came bearing cost you nothing?"

"Yeah, but if you don't want it or my company, I can leave now."

Roger smiled. "You can stay, as long as the beer does."

"I see you're your old, normal, annoying self. What are you up to today?"

"I was goin' through some stuff I brought with me from up north. Found it in my truck buried in the back behind the seat. I thought I'd lost everything, but there it was. Reminded me of something." Roger stopped. "Got time for a story that came to mind?"

"True or not?"

"I'll let you decide."

Bill said, "Okay, go for it. I'm all ears. I knew K9 wasn't the only one around here with a tale, pun intended. Go ahead. Indulge me."

"Well, you know how my life was fallin' apart when I lived up north?"

"Enough. Your wife and son died in an auto accident, and then you got booted out of your job at the university."

Roger said, "Yeah, and I hit rock bottom. I was so depressed and wanted to die. I tried to drink myself to death. One night, I ran out of alcohol around the house and went to a local bar to continue. I bellied up to the bar and was soon feelin' no pain. About a half hour and several drinks later, a bunch of bad news bikers came in, and the place got very rowdy. They started tryin' to pick fights, but no one wanted to fight. I sat there starin' at my drink, hopin' they'd get bored and go away.

"But no. The biggest, ugliest, and meanest lookin' biker started pickin' on me. I tried to ignore him, but he shoved me, grabbed my drink, and gulped it down. He said menacingly, 'Now whatcha gonna do about that?'

"I shook my head and said, 'Wish you wouldn't have done that. Today's the worst day of my life, and I think you need to listen to my story.' He looked at me strangely and laughed. 'Okay, buddy,' he said. 'You got my attention. Spill the beans.'

"I cleared my throat and said, 'I just lost my wife and son. Then I lost my job unfairly. I've hit rock bottom. I came in this bar tryin' to work up the courage to put an end to all my misery. I put a poison pill in my drink and watched it dissolve, but before I could drink it, you showed up and drank the whole thing. Now, as I see it, you and your gang have two choices. You can beat me up and even kill me, but I wanted to die, anyway. Of course, if you delay and do that, you probably won't make it to the hospital in time to have your stomach pumped and live. Your gang could clear the way. If you run all the lights, you should make it. What's your choice?'

"His face grew pale. He yelled and got his group's attention. 'We're out of here, now! I got to get to the hospital!' They emptied out the bar at a dead run, and the place grew quiet. Everyone was lookin' at me. I smiled and said, 'Time to go, bye,' and walked out the door. I never looked back.

"When I woke the next morning and found out I wasn't dead, I thought it might be a good idea to move to Florida that day or ASAP, which I did. Here, I resumed feeling sorry for myself and drinkin' heavily to kill the pain until you intervened and gave my life a little purpose." He paused. "Thank you. I may not be totally out of the woods, but I'm glad I didn't succeed in killin' myself. I had reason to live, and I didn't even know it."

They sat in silence for a few moments.

Bill said, "You're not the first one I talked down. Most people have a reason to go on. All do really, if you can only get them past the agony they're going through at that moment."

Several more moments passed in silence.

Bill said, "There's a lot more to you than meets the eye, Roger Pyles."

"You too, Bill Kenney. Thanks for thinkin' I was worth savin'. Now, are we gonna have a group hug or what?"

Bill cringed. "Not on your life."

"Good. I thought you might be goin' soft on me."

Bill swore under his breath. "Not on your life," he repeated, stronger.

"Double good. Now, what?"

"I want you to take the beer as partial down payment for what I've drank of your beer in the past."

"That's about a 1% down payment, you know."

Bill swore again and rose. "Think I better be going."

"Don't let the door hit you on the way out, ole buddy."

Bill gave Roger a dirty look to end all dirty looks.

Roger laughed. "Gotcha. Thanks, Bill, you're a good guy, even if I have to ruffle your feathers now and then."

"Hey, you know what goes around, comes around."

"Yeah, I know that. Thanks again, Bill. Enjoy the rest of your day."

"I will, ole buddy." He smiled, shook his head, and exited the porch, still smiling.

Roger watched as he walked to his truck and drove off. K9 came out from under the trailer. "Well, girl, that went well. No bloodshed and old tightwad Bill left beer. Will wonders never cease?"

She barked.

"My feeling exactly. He smiled. "It's good to have a purpose and be needed." His smile grew bigger. "And a few people in this world might even care for me. I think my life's gettin' better."

The End

WANT TO READ MORE?

Braddock's Gold Novels – Braddock's Gold, Hunter's Moon, Fool's Wisdom, and Killing Darkness

Florida Murder Mystery Novels – Death at Windover, Murder at the Canaveral Diner, Murder at the Indian River, Murder at Seminole Pond, Murder of Cowboy Gene, Murder in the Family, Murder the Most Dangerous Game, Going to the Dogs, and Can't Depend on Murder

Going to the Dogs is the eighth in the expanding *Florida Murder Mystery Novels*. Each book in the series is written as stand-alone novel. Readers say he keeps getting better. All of Mr. Heavner's twelve books can be found on Amazon as ebooks and paperbacks. The first book, *Braddock's Gold*, is also available as an audiobook from Audible at Amazon.

WANT TO HELP THE AUTHOR?

If you enjoyed the book, would you help get the word out? Please tell others about it. Word-of-mouth advertising is the best marketing tool on this planet.

A good review on Amazon, Goodreads, or elsewhere would also help the author be able to keep writing full time. It doesn't have to be long. Thanks.

SIGN UP FOR JAY HEAVNER'S NEWSLETTER

With this, Jay will occasionally keep you informed with new books coming out and anything else special. Feel free to email him at jay@jayheavner.com. His website is www.jayheavner.com. He loves reader feedback.

www.ingramcontent.com/pod-product-compliance
Lightning Source LLC
Chambersburg PA
CBHW060919250626

47159CB00008B/3077